# Diamonds to

# Dust

D1417158

# M. J. Rutter

# Acknowledgements

I want to thank my husband Franie for all of his help with this novel. Not only has he been my ears, he has helped with a lot of suggestions especially when it comes to Cockney slang. Together with his father, Frank Rutter, they both helped me put this story together and have waited a long time for it.

As always I would like to thank my ever loyal readers and fans, you are amazing. A huge thanks to my friends and family for your support.

I am dedicating this book to my father-in-law. An amazing man who has had to overcome more than most. Left fatherless he was raised by his mother in Poplar, East London and after being evacuated to Cornwall in the war, they settled in Bournemouth. He has served his country, he has been a boxer and he raised four children alone. The family has suffered its fair share of loss and I am in awe of one of the most amazing men I know, I am lucky to have him as my father-in-law and on top of all of that, if it weren't for him, I wouldn't have such an amazing husband.

Thank you, Frank, this is for you.

# One

A black BMW three series was being raced down the motorway driven by a young man with dusty blond hair and a dagger tattoo on his left arm. His eyes were an icy blue and his smile cheeky and confident, almost devilish like. In his chin he had a dimple and his lips made a perfect oval shape, succulent and soft. Beside him sat an attractive dark haired girl, with bouncy auburn curls and dark brown eyes. She gazed apprehensively over at him as they left the motorway and headed through the New Forest.

They were heading south, this was the beginning of their new life together, though she wished it had a better start. Woken sharply by a phone call, they were launched out of their bed in a warehouse loft in Poplar, East London.

Throwing as much as they could into bags and grabbing their passports in a panic, they forgot to lock up. As they raced towards Poole harbour and a ferry to Jersey their home had been visited.

"They're gone," s short stocky man with short cut grey hair, rolled his dusty blue eyes as he spoke into his phone. "Alright, boss, we'll catch 'em." He looked over at the other man; he was much taller with hardly any hair and a gap in his front teeth.

"I am too bloody old for this crap." The tall man groaned and kicked a pile of clothes across the wooden floor.

"He wants us to look around and see if they have any links." The shorter man said with his deep husky voice.

"Course he does." His friend groaned.

"Vic, we need this gig."

"No, Mason, you need this gig to pay for Charlie's wedding to that Pikey twat." he spat angrily.

"Well, what about your holiday anyway? I'm giving you half, ain't I?"

"Yeah, so you say. Look, did you know he has told all the boys at the King that he's taking her back to Dublin with him?"

"No he ain't." Mason groaned.

"We'll see, now let's have a look around this shit hole and go and get some breackie, bloody seven o'clock on a Sunday morning…" Vic grumbled rubbing his belly.

ཊཊཊ

"You should have told him to sling his hook in the first place." She snapped angrily.

"Well, you wanted to go to sodding America and I had to get the readies from somewhere to pay for it." He retorted sarcastically.

She shook her head, disbelieving his harsh accusation, "You said we could go and I thought you had the money for it, alright? So, don't blame me for this, Ben, this is not my fault." She scolded.

"I know. Look, babe, I don't want to fight, we got away from them and all we have to do now is lay low for a couple of days until the boat leaves." He sighed with a frown, she couldn't help but warm to him when he pulled that little boy lost face that melted her heart.

"Let's just hope we have got away," she groaned. "I heard Jock Mackenzie is a nasty bastard and the last idiot to rip him off lost his thumbs."

Ben smiled slightly, "Lisa, I think you'll find that was his plums. Look we will be alright, babes, I got connections. Let's get to your mum's house and I can make some calls."

"I hope so," she sighed gazing at the trees whizzing by, "this is scary, Ben and I don't like having to just leave everything because of this, we can never come back."

"I know." He said as he took her hand and kissed the back of it. "Bloody hell! When did they lower the speed limit here?" he asked and jammed the brakes on, they were both thrown forward slightly in their seats. "Sorry, I don't want to get a speeding ticket."

They arrived outside her mother's three bed council house in Kinson, a small part of the seaside resort Bournemouth. She could hear her brother's music as she climbed out of the car. This was her home, where she grew up and it was hard to accept she may never see it again or her family for that matter. Although she couldn't wait to move to London, this was still her home. All she had was her mum, brother and her Nan. It was going to be hard to leave them behind, but she knew she loved Ben and would do absolutely anything for him.

They had met two years previously in a night club in Soho called H2O. Ben Marshal caught her eye and she was hooked. His cocky arrogance attracted her more and when he gave her his number and said she would call him, she wanted to tell him to sling his hook, but she kept the number, just in case she changed her mind, of course she did. She liked him and fell for him instantly. A friend said he was dangerous and reckless and that made her more determined to make it work.

He came from The Smoke, as he put it, born and bred in the East End of London. He worked his way through school and with a head for numbers, he knew how to make his money work. He was an only child and his mum, an aging alcoholic, drove him to leave home at sixteen. He never knew his father; he was just in the other half of a torn photograph his mother gave him when he asked her where he was. He worked at a local supermarket for two years and then behind a bar in one of the West End casinos. That's when he met Lisa, the love of his life.

At first he thought she was this stupid, little girl with a crush on him, he'd met plenty of those. But this one was different, she did call him, but only to say what a cocky, little shit he was and if he didn't call her back in ten minutes, then she would know she was right about him. He had to call her, she challenged him and he liked that.


"I need to charge my phone." He said following her up the garden path.

"We can do it here, Mum won't mind." She replied. She opened the front door. "Hello?" she called out. There was some thumping from upstairs.

"Christ, look what the cat dragged in." Her brother Nick shouted over the banister. "Shit the bed or what?"

"Shut up you twat, where's Mum?" she asked.

"She's gone to Nan's," he continued as he walked down the stairs. "So, what do we owe for this pleasure?"

"We're moving away, so I thought I'd come and see you before we go." She explained.

"Oh, and where will that be then?"

"None of your bloody business, Nick," she snapped and marched through the house. "What time did Mum leave?"

"She won't be long," he looked at Ben.

"Oh, Ben, this is Nick, my twat of a brother I told you about."

"Cheers, sis," Nick frowned. "How the hell do you put up with her, mate?" Ben just smiled.

Nick made them both tea and shortly her mum came home. After hugs and a thousand questions, they had another cuppa and sat in the living room with the gallery of school photographs over the mantel. Her mum looked well and had bleached her hair again for the summer. The sun shone in rays and reflected of the crystal ornaments on the wall unit at the back of the lounge.

"You should have called me, love; I only got a small bit of beef at the shop."

"It's alright, Mum; I don't eat red meat anyway," Lisa replied.

"I'll put it in some gravy, it will go further that way. Did you peel the spuds, Nick?"

"I forgot," he groaned.

"Tell you what, Lisa, he ain't half a lazy git nowadays, don't get up much before twelve most days." She moaned.

"Nothing changes does it, Mum?" she smiled. "I'll do the spuds for you," Lisa and her mum went to the kitchen.

"So, when do you leave?"

"Wednesday, we are catching a ferry," she replied absently.

"To where, I thought you said you were moving?"

"We are, just got some things to sort out first. Ben has family in Jersey," she explained, her heart throbbing with more lies.

"I could see he was rich, he's a nice boy, love."

"I know," she smiled. If only she could tell her mum the truth. She was scared and couldn't tell a soul. "It's okay for us to stay 'til then though, right?"

"This is your home, Lisa, of course it's alright. Ben will sleep in your room I take it."

"Mum, I'm twenty-two, I know what I am doing, and we've been living together for eighteen months." She smiled.

"I know, love. I think I might make a crumble, Ben likes puddings, doesn't he?"

"Who doesn't," Lisa grinned.

ʊʊʊ

"Boss, I think they've gone down south, looks like his misses has a Nan in sunny Bournemouth." Mason explained into his phone.

"Well then, laddie, you had better get going then, hadn't you?" The cocky Scots voice on the other end replied. "I'll get two of my boys meet you at Fleet services. Call me when you have found him."

"Will do, boss," Mason hung up his mobile. "Vic, my old mate, hope you got your swimming trunks, we are off to the seaside."

"Great," Vic moaned, "I bloody hate sand."

"You're always bloody moanin', Vic." Mason complained opening the door to the car. Vic climbed in beside him.

"What do you expect? I had my arse dragged out of bloody bed on a Sunday mornin' to chase some cocky, little shit to the sodding beach. I'm nearly sixty, Mason and what have I got for my retirement? Fuck all. No pension for a Heavy, is there?"

"Didn't you put some away?"

"What, with my strife, you have to be joking, mate. She spends more money than the Queen. I ain't got a pot to piss in and she's shoppin' at Harrods for bikinis and sun lotion for a soddin' week in Marbella that I can't even afford to pay for."

"You do make me laugh, mate," Mason smiled.

ʊʊʊ

Lisa loved her mum's Sunday roast, even if she didn't like beef, it was just nice being at home and sat around the table. Nick took off out after lunch and never even helped with the washing up, so Ben and Lisa did it. She then took him to her room while her mum went to the neighbours to call her Nan. Her mum didn't have a phone and would not use a mobile.

"So, this is your room," Ben beamed and flopped down on the bed. The walls were covered with posters of Take That and her favourite movies like 'The Lost Boys' and Stephen King's 'It'. "You never told me you like horror films." He frowned.

"You never asked," she smiled. "God, what a mess?" she sighed as she gazed at her room, piles of old clothes and books on her chair and floor. "I might have a bath, actually."

"Now that sounds good," Ben pulled her into him.

"Forget it, Ben, my mum has radar hearing, you won't be able to as much as breathe on me here, she won't have it."

"Well, we better be quick then." He grinned alluringly.

"How can you be so calm, for all we know Mack's men could be on their way?" she frowned.

"Why? They don't know where you used to live," he smiled confidently.

"But they might ask Melanie or Stacey," her two friends from the office where she worked back in London.

"Nah, we're alright here, babe, I promise you," he pulled her in close to him and pressed his lips to her sensitive neck.

"Haven't you got some calls to make?" she smiled and pushed him back.

"Yeah, I suppose so," he sighed, "I am so tired though," he yawned and stretched showing her his flat stomach and jeans hanging from his waist.

"You can have a nap if you want, I am having a bath."

"Have you still got it on?" he asked.

"Yeah," she grimaced; it hurt her and rubbed under her arms.

"Well, put it back on after, won't you?"

"Yes, Ben," she frowned and went to the bathroom.

ᗯᗯᗯ

"We're in trouble now, mate," Vic chuckled as they walked across the car park, "it's only the Men in Black." Mason snickered as they approached them.

"Are you Mackenzie's boys?" Mason asked two men dressed in black trousers and black shirts, leaning against a black Range Rover with tinted windows. They both nodded yes. "Well, I am getting some coffee and Vic here needs a Gypsy's, so we'll be back in a minute." They nodded again.

"Talkative pair ain't ya?" Vic smiled and followed Mason into the services. "I'll tell you what, mate, they're getting' younger all the time, how are we gonna compete with 'em?"

"Experience speaks in volumes, Vic, me old mucker, volumes. Our rep is worth more than anything they 'ave done so far, we 'ave the gift of knowledge."

"Yeah, and a weak prostate where you have to piss every twenty minutes," Vic laughed for the second time that day.

ထထထ

"Nan's coming up for tea, love, she can't wait to see you," Lisa's mum called through the bathroom door.

"That's great, mum, I was going to see her later anyway," Lisa replied and climbed out of the lukewarm water. She had dozed off and her mum's knock had woken her. Ben was snoring his head off on her bed, she dressed quickly and went down to her mother, she had put the kettle on again. "You drink too much tea."

"What else have I got, love? I don't go out, not even to bingo now. I don't drink and I don't smoke anymore. All I have is tea. Is lover boy asleep?"

"Yeah, we got up early this morning."

"You look tired, sweetheart, are you alright?"

"Yeah, I'm fine, honest," she swallowed. She was far from fine, petrified that some heavy's were going to smash through the door, that they were going to hurt Ben. How could she sleep knowing all of that?

They talked the afternoon away, all about her friends and college. Ben and his pretend job, she couldn't tell her mum what he really did. Her mum filled her in on Nick's ex-girlfriends and the one that has his baby, a little girl called Mia. How her Nan had been ill and taken into hospital. It struck her that if anything happened to her Nan or her mum she wouldn't be able to come and say goodbye.

Her new life would consist of running, they wouldn't be able to stay anywhere for long, her life had jumped to a whole new level of complication and completely out of control now. She'd never get to meet her niece and defiantly would not have kids of her own, how could she? She couldn't drag them on the run with them. It wouldn't be fair.

# Two

ʊʊʊ

"Twenty-eight miles to sunny, sunny Bournemouth, Vic me old son," Mason beamed.

"I don't like the look of Tweedle Dee and Tweedle Dumb you know, mate," Vic sighed glaring through the rear view mirror at the black Range Rover closely following them. "They look like they've done some bird and ain't afraid to do more. I thought we just had to track this geezer down and take him back, looks like he wants this kid out of the picture, I am not going looking for some prepared graves, if you know what I am talking about."

"Look, Vic, I am here to do a job, no crap, no bull shit, no games. Jock Mackenzie is a mean arse fucker from Glasgow, I ain't about to turn down the readies, am I?"

"That's all you think about, ain't it? So, tell me this then, if you get stitched up for this and end up in the Scrubs for murder, how are you going to go to Charlie's wedding then? If this gets out of hand, I am off. I don't give a fuck what Jock wants."

ʊʊʊ

Ben returned from the bathroom, Lisa was sat on her bed, "Are you sure your mum is alright with me sharing your room? I don't mind kippin' on the sofa." He yawned and rested his head on her pillow.

"Ben, its fine, just no funny business, my mum doesn't approve of un-married sex in her house," Lisa smiled. "So, what did Rory say?" she asked after their Irish contact.

"He will be in Dublin with the passports two days from now. Then we can get a flight to the States."

"Then what? I mean, can you trust these contacts over there?" she asked.

"I bloody hope so, or we are in Shit Street," he cuddled into her. "It'll be alright, babe, you'll see, my mate out there is a top geezer, we'll be fine," he then kissed the top of her head.

She closed her eyes shortly after; it hurt her to see her nan looking so old and frail that afternoon, as in the pit of her stomach she knew that she would never see her again. It took ages for her to fall asleep she still felt she had unfinished business to take care of too.

ထထထ

"We've been drivin' round this bloody place all night, Mason. I'm knackered, mate, can't we 'ave a kip and start again in the mornin'?" Vic asked and yawned.

"Yeah, I'll get a street map tomorrow."

"Good idea," Vic smiled. Mason climbed out to tell the others what the plan was.

Vic had known Ray Mason most of his life, they were at a boy's home together in the East end of London until they were sixteen and kicked out onto the street. They were both taken in by a man called Carlos Christos, a Greek gang lord that had connections with the Krays and a few other undesirable characters around at that time. At first he gave them a job delivering packages, they had no idea what was in them and in return he gave them a roof over their heads, money in their pockets and another job at his boxing gym. He also gave them free lessons so they could protect themselves. In the early seventies both of them were sent to Borstal for being a little too light fingered in the local shops. They beat up a drug dealer for selling bad stuff, killing three kids on the estate. They were caught and convicted of petty theft and assault.

Borstal was a cynical detention centre when they got there; you had to fight for everything, even a bit of toilet paper. They witnessed beatings and rapes; they were involved with a few fights themselves. But a lad called Jonny Bean, better known as Beano, took them under his wing and looked out for them. He was built like a brick shit-house and had a whole gang working under him. Both Vic and Ray were grateful that neither of them wanted to be subjected to violations that took place during the night, where even the screws would turn a blind eye. If it meant they worked with Beano, then so be it.

They were eighteen when they were released a lot tougher and a lot more street wise. Time inside had woken them up and both decided to never go back if they could help it. Carlos was waiting for them and they went back to work for him. They had nothing else. Ray heard that his mum had moved up north with her new husband and Vic never knew what happened to his mum and sister. It bugged him, but like a lot of things in his life, he pushed it to the back of his head and kept it locked up.

Vic met Sheila in nineteen seventy four at a party in one of the clubs and they married later that year. She fell pregnant almost the first time they had sex behind one of the casinos where she worked as a barmaid. Vic did the only thing he thought was right and married her, but sadly she lost the baby at seven months and for a while no one could talk to him, not even his best friend. His bubbly, bleach blonde bombshell had reduced herself to a tired looking housewife in months. Then things all of a sudden started to get better, she started to wear makeup again and have her hair done.

They lived in a small flat above a launderette. The walls were black with mildew and when Carlos came to visit he was so disgusted he found them somewhere else, he was appalled to think that they lived in such squalor.

By this time Ray had also found a nice girl to marry, Monica and they lived next door to Vic in a high rise block near Poplar. A year after Vic's baby died, Sheila fell pregnant again and they had a beautiful baby girl that Christmas, she named her Michelle and Vic idolised his daughter.

They had two more children shortly after, a boy they named Steven and another girl called Sarah. They stayed in that little, two bedroom flat for years. The money Vic bought in was good, but not good enough to get them out of there. Ray just had the one, a girl called Charlotte and that was enough for him. Ray's wife Monica came from Italy and had jet black hair. She and Sheila had become the best of friends until Ray was given a house. Sheila not only missed her friend, but felt let down after all they had three kids in that flat, not just one.

Finally the council moved them to their own house on a new estate later that year, but the strained friendship between their wives was never the same. Sheila resented the money Monica flashed around, both men earned the same as heavies for Carlos, but Monica only had one child to spend it on. Ray managed to take his family abroad twice a year and Vic could only afford a holiday camp in Devon. Vic learned how easy it was to switch off to her moaning and just to keep working to bring in more money and keep her happy. He loved her more than life, but she was driving him crazy.

Vic's first daughter Michelle, married almost right out of school to a smart arse accountant and moved her to Chigwell, Steven went to university in Ipswich. He was so intelligent, he met a girl down there and after Uni. had finished he married her. Sarah worked as a bank clerk and as long as she had money coming in she was happy. Charlotte Mason had never worked, like her mother she planned to let her man keep her.

So much for Ray's luck, his only child fell for a boxing Pikey. Nothing in Vic's eyes could be worse. They had a job to understand him half the time. She met him at a pub after at a bare knuckle brawl set up by Mason and Vic. Sean Kelly came from a huge family in Dublin and on a weekend trip home with Charlie two weeks later he asked her to marry him.

Now she wanted the huge white wedding and Ray hadn't got the money to pay for it. So when Jock

Mackenzie offered them both hard cash for this job, neither of them could afford to turn the job down. Although Vic wasn't actually getting paid himself, Mason offered him some cash and with the all-important trip to Marbella coming up, how could he refuse?

# Three

Lisa woke with a startle; she'd had a nightmare about Jock and his goons beating Ben within inches of his life. She knew what he was doing was nothing short of psychotic, but she loved him, how could she not support him? Besides, what else did she have to look forward to? As soon as she finished college she left home and headed for the Smoke.

Bournemouth had outlived itself in her eyes and became nothing more than a retirement village and she was not about to wait for her pension. Out of season jobs were hard to find and the cost of living as expensive as London, but one thing drove her to the Smoke more than anything else, she wanted to go to the States, to start a whole new life and Ben was giving her that chance. She thought by working in London she'd find an American and they'd run away together, instead, on a girls night out she met Ben and fell for him instantly. Now he had the chance of giving her the dream she'd longed for. This was it and as much as it hurt to leave, she knew she wanted this, she needed it.

She wrapped her dressing gown around her and went to the kitchen. Her mum was sat over a cup of tea; she smiled as Lisa sat opposite her at the table. She poured her a cup from the steaming pot and frowned as Lisa added two tea spoons of sugar and milk.

"You make me laugh," her mum said. "A body of a super model and you eat sugar like there is no tomorrow."

"You know I can't drink it without sugar," Lisa yawned. "You're up early then?"

"I always am, there is something nice about sitting in your kitchen, in the peace and quiet in the morning, listening to the birds outside and your brother snoring," she smiled again. "But you are never normally up this early, girl."

"I am now; I normally start work at eight."

"How is the high flying job at that magazine then?"

"Mum, I work in the post room, it's hardly high flying," she sighed.

"But its bloody good money love or you wouldn't be able to visit like this."

"I suppose not," she frowned.

"And a holiday in Jersey, that's expensive," she added.

"Who told you we're going to Jersey?" she panicked.

"You did, said you had things to sort out and going to see Ben's family, he really loves you."

"I know," she smiled and sipped her sweet, warm tea. "What else did Ben say?"

"Not much, do you want a full English?"

"No mum, toast is fine." She smiled.

"I don't mind cooking for you, I bet Ben would like it."

"I expect he will; I'll go and ask him, okay?"

"Take him a cuppa." Her mum told her before rooting through the fridge and pulling out bacon and eggs.

She poured him a cup of tea and went to her room to wake him, he was at up in bed talking on the phone, his eyes looked troubled. She frowned as she sat on the end of her bed.

"Alright, thanks for letting me know, mate," he hung up and looked at her. "Did you keep the letters your Nan sent you in a box in the wardrobe?" he asked.

"Yes, shit, they've found out where we are, haven't they?"

"I don't know, babe," he pushed off the cover and sat beside her, she handed him the tea.

"They'll go to my Nan's house, Ben, she's on her own," her eyes filled with tears.

"Look, there's a Seacat going at twelve instead of four; we'll get the earlier one."

"What if they hurt my Nan?" she frowned and felt sick.

"She'll be alright, babe," he promised.

"She is seventy three, with a bad heart, she'll tell them where my mum is and everything."

"Well, call her and tell her we're leaving for Jersey at four from Southampton, that'll put them off the scent," he pulled his jeans over his boxers. "By the time they figure it out, we'll be gone."

"What if they hurt her though, to get to me?"

"They won't," he shrugged. "Tell your Nan we are moving to Spain, but haven't told anyone, so, to keep it surprise."

"Spain?" she frowned, hardly able to think.

"Yeah, by the time Jock has searched the whole of Spain, we'll be in Vegas living the high life," he smiled.

"I am so scared, Ben." He put his arm around her.

"Your Nan is tough, she survived the war." He assured.

"Yeah, but only because she used to sell stuff on the black market and had her own protection racket," she smiled and wiped her frightened tears. "She's not stupid though, she'll spin them a line, I know that much."

"Go and ring her," he kissed her cheek, "don't worry, babe, it will all be fine."

"I hope you're right," she stood.

Lying to her Nan was not going to be easy, after all, the woman had been around a long time and she knew her granddaughter very well. She'd had three daughters and knew all the tricks in the book. Nothing in Lisa's voice could let her Nan know how much danger she was really in for her own sake.

"Hi, Nan, its Lisa," she said and sat on her mum's bed.

"Hello, love, to what do I owe this pleasure?"

"Just wanted to tell you something, something I can't tell Mum or Nick yet, it's a secret and no one is supposed to know, so promise me you won't let on."

"'Course I won't, you know me. You're not up the duff are you?"

"What? No, of course not," she licked her nervous lips. "No, Ben and I aren't coming back, we're leaving for Jersey today at four, we're getting the ferry from Southampton and then we're moving to Spain, we are going to run a bar."

"That's fantastic, love, but why all the secrets, your mum is proud of you no matter what?"

"I know," she blinked and a tear fell.

"It's that boy isn't it, is he in trouble?" she asked.

"No, Nan, he's not," she lied and wiped her tears with a quivery hand.

"He looks shifty to me; you'd do well to keep him at arms-length, love."

"Nan, honestly, you don't trust anyone, do you?" she chuckled nervously.

"Nope," her Nan smiled, "just go careful, Lisa. I had some heavy looking blokes here first thing this morning, told 'em to sling their hooks, so whatever it is you and Ben are mixed up in, your secret is safe with me, alright?"

"If they come again, call the police," Lisa frowned.

"If they come again, they'll get my walking stick wrapped round their ear-holes. I can look after myself, love."

"I know, Nan, I love you."

"You too my sweetheart," her nan hung up the phone and Lisa returned to Ben, they had to book in by eleven ready for departure at mid-day.

Lisa gave her mum fifty pounds to go shopping with and Nick twenty to go and meet his mates in town. She wanted them both out of the way in case Jock's men came round or they had to watch them leave. She then wrote them a note saying that they were leaving from Southampton at four, Ben had messed the booking up. So, they had to go and they'd be in touch. They packed the few things they had and headed for the docks.

In the ferry terminal they sat near the window, Ben's car sat outside, he was sorry to be leaving it behind, but knew once he got to the States he could have a bigger and better car. Lisa drank bottle after bottle of cola and as a result took many trips to the toilet. She was so scared, she knew that once they got on the boat that was it, they were free, but they still had that hour sat there waiting.

Ben went outside for a cigarette, his hands shook violently, he knew he could pay with his life for what he had done to Jock and that no man had ever got away with ripping him off before. In a flash two black cars, a Jag and a Range Rover sped into the car park; Ben clocked them immediately and nodded to Lisa who watched from the window. She pushed the back pack behind the rubbish bins and came outside. Ben opened his car door and they both climbed in.

He started the engine as the Jag stopped in front of them, Mason and Vic climbed out. Ben slammed the car into reverse and wheel spun back as far as he could, he whipped the steering wheel around, but the Range Rover stopped him going any further, the younger men then also climbed out. Ben put up his hands as if he were being arrested.

"Stay in the car," he said to her and climbed out. The two men grabbed him and dragged him around the side of the building. Mason and Vic nodded at Lisa and she climbed out.

"Well, well, well, look who it ain't," Mason growled. Vic hated it when he did this, acting all cocky. *Twat*! "So, leaving the country then were ya?"

"No, we're going on holiday."

"Oh yeah, we heard ya, love, talkin' to ya nan, off to sunny Spain then, only, we checked the bookings and look what we found."

"What?" she frowned. "We are waiting to sail at four." She insisted.

"We know you are going at twelve and we are quite happy to let you." Vic added and wiped the sweat off his forehead with a white hanky. "Just give us Jock's goods and you can go."

"Who the fuck is Jock?" she snapped.

"Look, there is no need to use that language, I'm not swearing, am I?" Vic continued, "They will kill him, love, just hand it over."

"I don't know what you're talkin' about," Ben grunted out in pain, obviously getting the hiding of his life.

"I can stop all of this," Mason reasoned. "We just want the stuff and we're gone."

"What stuff?" she demanded.

"Lisa, isn't it? You are a smart girl, I know it. Vic here knows it and Ben knows it too, but you are not being very smart right now, poppet."

"Yeah right, well, if I knew what you were after I would give it to you, but I also know that as soon as I do, you will kill us anyway," she retorted.

"That's not how it works," Vic replied. One of the younger men came over out of breath.

"He ain't squealin', call Jock and find out what he wants next," he ordered Mason.

"Taking your orders from monkeys now, my, you must really love your job," Lisa snarled.

"Look, sweetheart," the guy frowned, "if you are prepared to watch him die over this, then that's your priority, but after we're done with him, you can only imagine how much fun we're gonna have with you," he then smiled and wiped blood from his knuckles on a white handkerchief, Mason dialled a number and walked away.

Vic began to feel for this girl, she was the same age as his daughter, Sarah and wondered how he'd feel if she was in the same situation. Lisa glanced over at Ben, he lay in a heap on the ground and the other thug kicked him and smiled at her. Her heart was screaming give it to them, but her head told her to keep her mouth shut. She wondered why the security officers weren't calling the police; at least they'd stop this. Mason returned and two security guards came out of the check in building.

"Down the back," Mason frowned. The other heavy grabbed Lisa's arm and dragged her towards Ben. He was trying to get up, his white shirt and beige jeans were drenched in his own blood, he looked up at her, as tears began to stream down her cheeks. "We can stop this, look you're kids, he just wants them back."

"The bag," Ben frowned and looked at Lisa, "they're in the bag."

"And I thought you Cockney boys were tough," the other thug growled.

"It's inside," Lisa explained quietly.

Vic escorted her into the building and she pulled the bag from behind the bins. Back outside she pulled a small black bag from the back pack and handed it to Vic. He looked inside and nodded at the thugs.

"Got 'em," he smiled, "clever girl."

"Don't patronise me," she snapped and fell to the ground to help Ben.

"So, what do we do with 'em now?" the first thug asked.

"Let 'em go, we're not into lead weights and all that, boys," Mason smiled. "You have hurt the kid; he is going, let them go. He won't mess with Jock again."

"But he normally…"

"Lisa, take Ben and get out of here," Vic frowned, "you kept your side, I'll keep mine."

"What?" the thug glared at Vic.

"There are cameras and videos all over this place, mate; you want to go down for murder, you are on your own. You got what you came for." Vic winked at Lisa.

"But, Jock…"

"Jock is a jumped up Scot with no bollocks; you want yours to fry for him? He wouldn't piss on you if you were on fire." Mason turned to them, "Go on you two, get him cleaned up, they won't let you board like that." Lisa helped Ben to his feet. She glared into Vic's eyes as she passed him, he saw his daughter in her and respected her for that.

Once safely inside she supported him under his arm as he tried to walk. "Lisa, go and say I was jumped or something, they'll let us bored and get us some help," Ben groaned as she sat him on the seat. She raced over to the customer service counter.

"Excuse me, my boyfriend has just been mugged in the car park, can you help me?" she asked the blonde girl.

"Oh, my God, yeah, uh, Jeff knows first aid, can he walk? Do you want me to call the police?"

"No, no he said they didn't get anything, we really need to get the boat."

"Oh, you will," she smiled, "Jeff, can you help these two, he's been mugged?" she asked a man with his back to them, he turned and frowned.

"Bloody hell, mate, look at the state of you." Jeff smiled, he had fiery red hair and a face full of freckles.

"I can't miss the boat," Ben moaned.

"You won't, we'll get you boarded early."

He promised as he led them to a room with a bed and dressed Ben's many wounds, his lip was cut, his eyes were black and blue. Ben felt like he'd been hit by a bus, but he couldn't let on, they still had to get out of there quick.

True to his word, Ben and Lisa were boarded by Jeff at eleven thirty and he provided them with a complimentary lunch. As soon as the boat left the harbour, Lisa closed her eyes in Ben's arms and drifted off to sleep. They had evaded them this time, but deep down she knew Jock was not about to give up that easily.

They arrived in St. Hellier, Jersey and had one day before the flight to Dublin. Ben found them a bed and breakfast near the airport and as soon as they got to their room the both breathed a sigh of relief. She worried about her Nan and her mum, wondering if she'd ever forgive her for leaving without a goodbye.

After a well-deserved shower they headed out for a meal where the dined on salmon and champagne. They took a slow romantic walk back to their room and went to bed. Ben's head pounded, she gave him two pain killers and kissed him goodnight.

"Love you, babe," he yawned.

"Love you too, Ben." she replied and drifted off to sleep snuggled up behind him.


The toilet flushing upstairs woke her sharply, she sat up. Ben still slept facing the window, so quietly she climbed out of bed and crept into the bathroom. She took another hot shower and wrapped a towel around her body, Ben was sleeping still and they had to be down stairs for breakfast at nine.

"Ben," she called drying her body. "Ben, you gotta get up, babe." He didn't move. She pulled her dress over her damp body and sat on the bed behind him. "Ben," she kissed his shoulder and it felt cold to her lips. "Ben, come on." He still didn't move. She pushed her hands under the covers and stroked his leg, it also felt icy cold. "Ben, come on." She climbed over him, his eyes were wide open and he was glaring into space. "Ben," she swallowed. "Ben, stop messing around." Still nothing. Her eyes filled with tears, "Come on, baby, we got to get up." She brushed her tears away, "please." He just stared. She ran to the door, "Someone, help me," she screamed. The hotel owner came running up the stairs. "I can't wake my boyfriend."

"Let me see," the owner said. She stood at the door, he looked at Ben, pressed his fingers under his chin and then looked back at her. "I'm so sorry," he frowned, "I'll call an ambulance."

Within a few moments, or so it seemed, the ambulance had come and pronounced Ben as dead, he had most likely died from multiple bleeds inside, they took his body to the mortuary and she was now alone. She couldn't go home and she couldn't call anyone. The hotel owner was a lovely man and looked after her with sweet tea and comforting hugs, but all she wanted was Ben. His mobile began to ring in her room; it was his friend from Dublin.

"Hello?" she said."

"Hi, is Ben there?" he asked, his tinny accent was ripe and sounded harsh to her ears.

"He's uh, he's dead," she sniffed.

"Shit, no! Did they get him?"

"Yes they did," she swallowed.

"Oh, Lisa, I am so sorry, are you coming on your own?"

"What?" she frowned, confused.

"You have to come; they could come looking for you," he insisted.

"But I can't do this on my own," she mumbled.

"Look, get that flight at three. I'll meet you, you are not on your own," he'd already been paid for his help. Ben had been friends with Rory O'Connor for years.

"What about Ben's body? I don't know what to do." She moaned.

"Just be on that plane, love, we'll work it out," she hung up Ben's phone and realised they could trace it so she snapped the sim card and smashed the phone into pieces. She left the hotel with her bags and a few belongings of Ben's.

She took his passport and his wallet, tucked them into his backpack and threw it into a large bin before crossing the street to the airport. She had taken his St. Christopher from his neck before they took his body and with it pressing against her chest, she boarded the plane bound for Dublin. That night she would be flying to America, (;) destination un-known. Ben wanted to hit Vegas, but she just wanted to curl up and disappear forever.

She remembered Rory from a party and dived into his arms as he met her in Dublin. She sobbed in his arms as they sat in the back of a taxi. He had icy blue eyes and long eyelashes, his brown hair was curly and he needed a shave. In his flat he handed her a glass of Whiskey, she hated it, but knew it would help.

"I have booked you on a flight for Boston; I have sorted out a contact there for you." He handed her a new passport containing a Visa, "For this flight you are Bryony Lynch, and you are from a small Irish village called Bally near Cork, but you grew up in England, okay?" She nodded, not sure she liked the name Bryony. But it was a start. "The contact is called Rex and will meet you at Logan," he then handed her a wad of American cash. "There's three grand there and that should get you to Houston. You'll have three days to get there and that's where a guy called Mark Hobbs will take them off you, he has ten Million dollars there waiting for you. When you get to Houston, get a gun."

"Why?"

"In case he tries to screw you over," he replied. She wouldn't know if she was being screwed over.

"Can't you come with me?"

"Do you want me to?" he asked.

"I'd feel better if you did, just until I made the drop, I'll pay you." She sighed as tears filled her eyes again.

"Okay," he nodded, "well, I did book a ticket for me too, just in case."

"Thank you, Rory, I don't know what else to do," she sniffed.

"You go and live your dream, yours and Ben's, he'd have wanted that.

# Four

After seven long hours in the air they landed in Logan, Boston. She was exhausted and Rory had been no help at all during the flight. All he did was talk about Ben and the antics they got into as kids.

When she closed her eyes she re-lived the nightmare back in Poole that felt like it was years away, not just the day before. She missed him desperately and ached to be in his arms again. But she couldn't go back, he was gone and she had to go on.

The immigration officer looked her up and down over the rim of his glasses, he had silver hair and ebony skin with huge, warm brown eyes.

"So, what part of Ireland are you from?" he asked her.

"Uh, Bally," she replied trying out an Irish accent. "It's a small village near Cork."

"I took the wife a few years back, went to Dublin and Rosslaire."

"Ah yes, I know it well," she smiled.

"Never seen a green like it," he smiled. "So you are going to be studying up in Maine?" she looked over a Rory he nodded.

"That's right, thought I'd try it out."

"Well, good luck to you, Bryony."

"Thanks," she smiled.

They collected their bags and headed out of the arrivals lounge. Rory led her outside, the sun felt warm and the air thick and humid, but a light breeze blew around her legs.

"Great take on the old Irish there, Lisa." Rory smiled. Lisa couldn't open her mouth through fear that they would arrest her any minute, she wasn't a good actor or a good liar for that matter.

"You're late," a short, Irish blonde with a tinny accent and huge brown eyes smiled.

"Rex," Rory grinned and threw his arms around her. "Did you get my message?"

"Yeah, I got it, you must be, Lisa...I mean...Bryony, sorry," she playfully slapped her forehead.

"Nice to meet you," Lisa smiled and shook her hand.

"Gees girl, you really have been through it, huh?"

"I suppose," Lisa sighed sadly.

"Well, come on then, let's get you two back to my place then you can hit the road."

"The road?" Lisa frowned.

"Yeah, we're driving to Houston," Rory explained "you sort of need ID here to fly, since nine-eleven anyways, so we're gonna hit the high way."

"Is Rex coming with us?"

"No, I have to work, but I have sorted a car out for you," she loaded their bags into the back of her Mercury and the headed into south Boston.

Rex drove them to her house, Lisa sat in the back with Rory as he explained quietly that Rex didn't know the real reason for her visit, but he did tell her about Ben dying, Rex had also known Ben from years back and was upset to discover his untimely departure. Hearing his name ripped at what was left of her heart, shredding at it, making it burn in her chest and almost suffocating her.

She rubbed her hands as she gazed out of the window watching the streets and high rises fly by. S*o this was America, Ben would have loved Boston* she thought to herself.

Rex had a small house down a street lined with trees. Outside sat a bright red Dodge Neon, and she informed then that this was their car. They loaded the car, Rory paid her and they left. It was going so fast, at least a three day drive would give her time to catch her breath. Just two days before she started the day in Ben's arms and thought nothing could go wrong. Now she was in America without him and he was lying cold in a fridge back in Jersey.

They hit the interstate and drove down towards New York. Rory told her to rest and she closed her eyes.

ಠಠಠ

"I don't believe this," Jock frowned and looked at Vic and Mason. He poured the contents of the bag on to his desk in front of him. "I have to congratulate you two on being the biggest pair of fuck up's I have ever used."

"What?" Vic frowned. Who was this short ginger haired, whiskey sipping, skirt wearing Jock to talk to him like that? "You wanted and we delivered."

"The thing is, Victor, you have delivered a bag of bloody glass. These are nothing but Cubics, not sodding diamonds, not ten million quid's worth of diamonds."

"Well, what the fuck do we know about bloody diamonds? You wanted them, they gave them to us. How do you know they were kosher in the first place?" Vic replied smartly.

"Because, you fat idiot, I had them checked, Ben was supposed to get the codes cleaned off them and he ran off with them. You have let the little shit go with my fucking gems."

"Who are you calling a fat idiot you short-arsed, red-nosed, tosser?" Vic roared.

"Calm down, Vic," Mason warned.

"No, Mason, I didn't want this gig, you did. I am done. I didn't know you wanted us to kill the little shit for you. Maybe you should grow some balls and take care of your own fuckin' jobs in future."

"Get out of my office now," Jock barked.

"Get out of my town you alcoholic, arrogant, jumped-up twat," he turned to Mason. "You want to work for this prick, be my guest. I don't work for dickless wonders anymore." Vic stormed to the door, "Cock-sure, know it all twat! Who the hell do you think you are?" he grumbled as he walked, then slammed the door behind him.

"He has just made a big mistake," Jock snarled.

"No, mate, you have. Vic is one of the most straight-up blokes I know, he never swears and you my friend have just pissed him off. Look, I have got connections in Jersey; I'll see what I can find out."

"You do that," he groaned as Mason headed for the door.

Vic was outside leaning against the wall smoking, his hands were still shaking with temper. Mason stood and glared at him. "Don't you bloody start," he ordered.

"I am not going to say a word," Mason shrugged.

"Yeah, good," Vic snapped and threw his cigarette on the ground.

"Is, uh, is Steve still in Jersey?" he asked casually.

"No way, mate, you are on your own." Vic growled and stormed off towards the car.

ʊʊʊ

The heat in Mississippi was too much for Lisa, it almost suffocated her. They had been on the road for almost two days and driven across five and a half states. Rory wouldn't even stop to eat, so he bought snacks and junk in the gas stations. He wanted to get to Houston, but they only had to get across Louisiana and into Texas. She marvelled at the different States, the shades of green in the trees and the brightest blue sky she had ever seen.

She'd hardly eaten, not a lover of junk food, especially if it had been in a hot car all day and night. Rory was worried about her, so he stopped at a restaurant on the highway so they could eat and have a rest. She could drive, but he wouldn't let her. He felt he owed it to Ben to get her there safely.

They ate a huge breakfast of bacon and eggs with grits and pancakes. She ate well and washed it down with hot coffee, although she'd have given anything for some tea.

They hit the Texas border early on the third day, the sun was hot at seven in the morning and they drove into Houston just after twelve. Rory stopped near the docs and pushed the car into the water, they then booked into a hotel where they showered and changed then waited for Rory's phone to ring to arrange meeting this Texan cowboy, Mark Hobbs. Lisa unpicked the stitching in her white lace Basque. She had kept it on, even though it hurt her to wear it, even though she was so hot, she still wore it, just as Ben had asked. They had spent hours sewing the diamonds into the underwear, now it was time to take them out of it.

"Wow, so that's where you hid them?" Rory smiled handing her a glass of juice.

"Thanks," she took the juice but had no intention of drinking it. "Yeah, well no one would think to look there." She placed the juice down and continued picking the diamonds from the lace. "So, this Hobbs bloke, is he alright?"

"Yeah, Mark is alright, loaded; he has more money than I could ever hope to have. He hates that Jock bastard too."

"Don't we all," she sighed. "Right, that's all of them," she pushed them into a pile. "Who'd have thought that these could be worth so much money?"

"I know," he smiled and for a split second thought about taking them all and running, but he owed Ben his life. He knew he had to get this done for Lisa, so she could live the life they should have had together.    Rory knew Mark was legit and trusted him as much as he did Ben, the three of them were friends after a summer in Dublin before Ben met Lisa. Ben stopped a ruthless gang lord from slitting Rory's throat and he promised to pay Ben back somehow. He knew Ben loved Lisa and would have walked over hot lava for her. He owed his friend and a promise is a promise.

Three o'clock on the dot, Rory's phone rang, the time was set and they headed across the sunny streets of Houston to an apartment block overlooking the docks. They took the lift to the penthouse suite and as the doors opened they were greeted by a man in a black suit. He smiled friendly and led them inside.

Mark Hobbs was almost six feet tall. Dressed in a white shirt and blue jeans with a brown leather belt and a large, gold buckle. He had a pure white smile and olive green eyes, a square jaw and was extremely handsome. He was sat with his long legs out stretched in front of him and crossed at the ankles. His tan leather Cowboy boots looked new and on the table sat a tall glass of clear liquid and ice. He stood with a warm smile as they approached him, Lisa caught a whiff of his expensive aftershave and it set her belly on fire.

"Rory, you old son of a gun," he announced loudly in a strong Texan accent, "I was so surprised to hear you had come too," he grinned and shook his hand.

"We ran into a little trouble back in the UK," Rory explained briefly.

"Oh, yeah, I am sorry about Ben. He was a good man," He lowered his eyes to Lisa, "And you must be the love of his life," he held his hand out to her.

"Hi," Lisa smiled and shook his hand, 'I'm Lisa and I *was* the love of his life, evidently, not anymore."

"Please, have a seat both of you, would you like some tea?"

"Yes please," she smiled.

"He means iced tea, Lisa; I don't think they make it hot here." Rory explained.

"Hey, if the lady wants hot tea, we can make her hot tea," Mark smiled and sat opposite her. "Please get the lady a nice hot cup of tea," he ordered. Then he looked at her sympathetically. "Can I ask what happened with Ben?"

"Uh, they caught up with us at the docks and they beat him up," she explained painfully. "He was fine when we got to Jersey and went to bed, and then he just…didn't wake up."

"Jesus, poor Ben," Mark frowned.

"Yeah," Rory scowled and looked at Lisa. She had turned white. "Do you have any news yet?"

"Yes, actually, I do, I have a buyer in Tokyo already, so, may I see the little ladies?" Mark asked.

"Yeah, sure," Lisa pulled the small velvet bag from her bag and handed it to Mark. He gazed inside and his eyes lit up. A hot cup of tea was placed in front of Lisa; she added milk and a sugar.

"They are beautiful. I agreed twenty with Ben, I hope that still stands."

"Yes, that's great," she smiled.

"Good, now what are you going to do, I believe you were planning on staying here in the US?" he asked.

"I can't go back," she sighed, "but I don't know what to do about Visas and stuff."

"I have a little place down in Austin; Texas is a big state, big enough to disappear in."

"It could be a start, Lisa," Rory suggested, "somewhere to lie low for a while. I mean, at least you can think about things."

"Are you sure? You don't even know me," she quizzed Mark.

"No, but I knew Ben, he was like a little brother as far as I am concerned. This makes you family." He replied with a slight smiled. "It's a nice house and there is a car there too. Just until you figure out what you want to do. No one knows about it, it's my little hideaway," he sipped his drink. "Then, when you are ready, I have an excellent lawyer, it will be nothing or him to rustle up a new identity for you both."

"That is very generous of you, Mr Hobbs." She smiled.

"Lisa, please, call me Mark."

"Okay, Mark, but to be honest, this Jock bloke is not just going to give up on these gems, he will come looking and the less people who know where I am the safer it will be for them."

"Well, how about a few days then, just until you can sort out the paperwork. This guy I know could have you new identities within a day or two." He smiled. Lisa thought for a moment, and then she nodded, "Okay, thank you, Mark, very much," she replied sweetly. He beckoned one of his men over and he placed a briefcase on the table.

"Now then, here is a million in cash as arranged and the rest will be transferred into the account before five today," Mark explained.

"What account?" Lisa frowned.

"Ben's uh, account, to transfer it to an account in your name you'll need a social security number, which you can't obtain until you have the correct paperwork." He then handed her some keys and smiled. "I'll have my lawyer call you in two days and make some arrangements for you."

"Can I trust you, Mark?" she asked gazing into his friendly eyes.

"Yes, you can," he replied. She looked at the stones, "Why don't you keep hold of these ladies until I can complete the transfer, if that will make you happier."

"Or maybe we could just stay here and meet your lawyer to arrange the new identities etcetera." Lisa suggested. "If that's alright with you though, I have had those things on me for days and the sooner I see the back of them the better. But…"

"I can understand how you feel you can't trust anyone, Lisa, I don't blame you either. I am a man of my word, but if you feel better staying here, then I would love the company," he smiled and stood. "I'll show you to the guest room, I only have one but I am sure Rory will cope on the couch."

"I'll sleep anywhere," Rory added, "thanks, Mark."

"No problem, any friend of Ben's, is a friend of mine."

ʊʊʊ

"Steve, me old mate, how the heck are ya?" Mason smiled as Vic drove them across London.

"Mason, you old fart, how are you, mate?"

"Got a bit if a problem to be honest."

"Let's have it then," Steve replied. Mason explained what had happened and he said he would call back. Mason closed his mobile phone with a snap. Vic let out a huge sigh.

"So, you are going to let that prick kill this kid then?"

"No, I want to find the little twat first, I'll get the gems and then he's off my back, alright."

"Do you know what, mate, I have always backed you up, but I can't on this, okay, so he took a few stones?"

"A few? Ten million quid's worth of gems is not a few, Vic," Mason snapped, "If you don't want ya fingers burned, you should leave fire well alone. He knew the risk he was taking, dragging that poor girl with him. I bet her family are worried sick about her."

"So, now it's the girl you are worried about?"

"Do you think Jock is going to leave her alone? No, he won't, when they find them, they will kill them both. Jock is a nasty bastard, Vic, he will not stop until they are both six foot under."

"Are we going to Jersey then?"

"I am, but you my friend, you are going home to the missus," Mason frowned.

"If he sends Tweedle Dumb and Tweedle Dee, what chance will you have against them?"

"Well, I am not sitting on a sodding boat listening to you moaning about being tired, or hungry, or tired and hungry."

"And I ain't letting you go on ya own, you have to give your girl away to that bloody Pikey next month and I am not doing it in your place."

"Right then," Mason smiled, "what do we tell the girls?"

"She ain't talking to me anyway, so I don't give a toss." He shrugged.

"So, I'll tell Monica I am out with you for the weekend."

"Oh, Sheila will love that, she'll kick me out on my arse," he moaned.

"You can always have the sofa at our gig if you want, mate," Mason added tapping him on the shoulder.

ⴲⴲⴲ

Mark arranged for more hot tea for Lisa while Rory left to get the bags. This tall stranger seemed nice enough, but could she really trust him or anyone now? She glared over the water in the pool, it looked so inviting in the evening sun. Mark felt a little on edge around Lisa, she was so scared and he didn't want to frighten her completely. He owed Ben so much, looking after Lisa was the least he could do.

When Rory returned she relaxed a little, Mark showed her to his spare room and she took a shower. The hot water felt so good on her tight stressed out body.

After, she dressed in a small, light green, cotton dress and Mark arranged for some food to be ordered in for dinner and she picked at her plate of chicken and salad.

"Don't you like it, Lisa?" Mark asked.

"I am not hungry to be honest," she replied.

"You must be, all that travelling," he smiled.

"No," she shook her head and looked at Rory.

"She hasn't eaten a lot since we met in Dublin," he explained.

"I will eat when I am hungry," she interrupted annoyed that they talked about her with her sat there.

"What about the ice cream? Everyone likes ice cream," Mark offered.

"Mark, I'm fine. I don't want any salad or ice cream and I don't want any more bloody tea, okay?" She stood and went to her room.

She felt bad for snapping but they must have realised how much pain she was in. Ben was dead; she couldn't even go to his funeral. Mark knocked on the door and pushed it open.

"I am *such* an ass," he said.

"No, you have been very nice, it's me," she admitted.

"Well, I just feel like I owe it to Ben to look after you," he said softly.

"I'm a big girl, I don't need looking after and I certainly don't need food rammed down my throat every two minutes. At home I'd eat once a day," she retorted.

He shrugged his broad shoulders and muttered, "Sorry."

"Do you have any booze?" she asked feeling bad for acting so childish, "I could really use a stiff drink."

"I have a bar, follow me," he replied and she followed.

ღღღ

"Mason, it's Steve, sorry, mate, I got some bad news for ya," he said in his ear.

"Go on," Mason groaned and looked at Vic.

"My lady friend works at the hospital. A Ben Marshal was bought in two days ago."

"Ah, so he's in hospital then," Mason smiled excited, "well, you go an 'ave a word with him."

"I would, mate, might be a problem though." Steve replied.

"Why? Just say you're his uncle or summin'," Mason shrugged.

"He uh, he can't talk, Mason."

"Steve, for a Uni graduate, you ain't the sharpest tool in the box, get to the point, son, eh?"

"He's brown bread, mate. I can't go and talk to him 'cos he's as dead as John Lennon."

"What, stone cold?" he shook his head, heat raced to his face and his shirt felt tight around his neck, they had killed that poor kid.

"Yeah, they only had his name because he was booked into a hotel; his girlfriend fled the scene and hasn't been seen since."

"Fantastic, that's just fan-fuckin'-tastic, cheers mate," he snapped as he slammed his phone shut and looked at Vic, he shook his head. "We'd better go and see Jock."

"Do you want to know something?" Lisa asked Mark as he poured her a glass of vodka and dropped ice cubes into it.

"Sure," he replied.

"I don't know what I am supposed to do now. Ben had all the answers, he knew exactly what he was going to do, so I left it up to him." Mark placed the glass in front of her. "It wasn't supposed to be like this," tears welled in her eyes.

"Hey, come on now. I know it's hard," he raced around the bar and sat beside her. "Look, Ben has always been what you Brits call a 'Jack the lad', I believe," he smiled slightly. "He knew what he was doing and the risk he was taking, don't forget that."

He sighed loudly, "And now I have all of this money and I don't know what to do with it."

"I can help you, Lisa, if you want me too. A sudden increase in finances can be as stressful as being broke." He explained. "You don't know who to trust, your friends will change towards you. The new ones will make you wonder if they are truly a friend or looking for a hand out," he sipped his whisky shot. "Look, don't make any rash decisions yet, okay? You wanted a new life and you have got one, the last thing you need is to panic, mistakes can be made when you do. Just remember you are not alone. I will help you as much as I can and Rory, well, he has nothing else anyway, I am sure he'll be sticking around for some time." She sipped the icy vodka and thought about Mark's kind words.

"So, what about Jock? What if he finds me, everyone I know will be in danger?"

"Lisa, how will he find you, honey? No one knows you are here, and this is a huge country, believe me, you can hide if you want to. I should know."

"What do you mean?" she frowned.

"Well, first off, my name is not Mark Hobbs and I was not born in Texas, but you didn't hear that from me. I just want to show you that you can trust me, Lisa," he smiled.

"So, can I ask what your real name is?"

"No," he replied bluntly.

"Oh," she replied surprised by his reaction.

"Oh, it's nothing like that, it's just a little embarrassing that's all," he explained and drank some more whiskey. "My lawyer friend is called Alex and he will be here at nine, we'll sort out this social security number so you can get on with living in your new life."

"You act like it's exciting," she grimaced.

Delight flashed in his eyes with his huge smile, "Oh, honey, it is, a whole new you, you could dye your hair and choose a new name."

"I do hate my name," she smiled, "but I am too dark to go blonde."

"This is America and with the right stylist you'd be surprised," he grinned.

After a few more drinks she went to bed, she found it easier to sleep that night. The first real sleep since Ben had died and as soon as her head hit the pillow she drifted off.

She woke feeling sick as soon as she opened her eyes. She ran to the bathroom and threw up. Her stomach swam and her head spun, she hadn't drank so much liquor since she left college, and had obviously lost her ability to consume insane amounts of alcohol without so much as a hangover to show for it. She washed her face and brushed her teeth, but as soon as she returned to her bed, she felt sick again so raced back to the bath room and knelt over the toilet.

Rory called through her door, "Are ye alright in there?"

"No," she groaned into the toilet bowl and began throwing up again.

After some time she was able to leave the bathroom and get herself dressed. Alex, the lawyer was waiting for her when she finally emerged. He had light coloured hair and gold framed glasses over his dusty blue eyes. Mark handed her a cup of black coffee and smiled.

"That premium stuff is pretty strong, sorry, Lisa, I should have warned you," he explained.

"I can normally handle my drink," she smiled slightly and sat at the table.

"This is my lawyer, Alex Stonebridge." Mark explained.

"Nice to meet you, Lisa," Alex said shaking her hand as she sat. She placed her coffee down and gave a friendly smile. "So, what I need to do first of all is take a picture for your new identity. Would you mind wearing eye glasses?"

"Why?" she frowned and sipped the coffee.

"Well, it's clichéd, but I thought it is better than cutting off your hair."

"Actually, I can do both," she nodded, "I just want to look completely different."

"I know a great hair stylist, Lisa, I'll call her now." Mark said lifting his phone. "The sooner we get this done, the sooner we can get your funds sorted out."

"So," Alex continued as Mark made a call. "I understand that you came over as a Bryony Lynch," she nodded yes, "You can't use that name anymore. As soon as that study visa is up, they will be looking for you. What would you like to be called now? I have a list of names for you to choose from. All we need is to add a picture to your driver's license and passport." He pushed the list to her and she glared at the many names, looking for something she could live with. Her best friend Shelly from school had a little sister called Holly and there was a name on the list, Holly Long, she pointed to it. "Okay, nice to meet you, Holly Long," he grinned.

"And I'll be safe, no one will know the truth?" she asked.

"As soon as you sign your new name on the documents, Lisa Wilkinshaw will no longer exist." He handed her a pen.

"I feel like I am signing my life away."

"You are, in a way," Rory smiled as she scrawled across the many papers.

Mark's hairdresser friend arrived shortly after. She cut and bleached Lisa's hair. Instead of the loose curls that she had to iron out almost every day, she now had jaw length hair, bleached into a realistic blonde and it made her brown eyes sparkle as she gazed at her reflection, almost a complete stranger now. She smiled and turned.

"Wow," Mark exclaimed with an excited grin, "you look…terrific."

"Thanks," she smiled again with colour rushing to her cheeks.

"Yeah, it suits you," Rory added as she lifted her purse from her bag.

"It's all taken care of," Mark said as he crossed the room. The stylist, called Jenna, smiled and left. "Alex's fees are also taken care of; you keep your money for you."

"I can pay my way, Mark," she grumbled.

"I know. But it's the least I can do," he insisted gazing into her eyes briefly and she looked away. "So, *Holly*," he emphasised, "you need to empty that bag of everything that links you to Lisa. I'll get my camera and we can get your pictures taken," he left the room.

"My name is now, Ethan Rhodes, kinda has a film star vibe going on there," Rory announced proudly.

"Sure does," she smiled and tipped her bag out on the coffee table.

"Wow Li…I mean, Holly," Rory smiled, "you have a lot of junk in that small bag."

"Yes I do," she frowned, she lifted a picture from her purse of Ben, he had that stupid Twenties Gangster costume on, the picture was taken on the previous Halloween. He was grinning smugly with a fake cigar in the corner of his mouth, they had so much fun that night and it burned her heart to see him again. Her eyes instantly filled with hot tears.

"You can't keep it," Rory said quietly, suddenly at her side, "sorry."

"I know," she sniffed and wiped her tears away. "It's fine, this is what he would have wanted."

"That's the spirit," he hugged her quickly, she stiffened at his touch, not because she didn't want him to, but it surprised her. She'd had no one really touch her since Ben and it caught her off guard. "Sorry."

"No, don't be." She tried to smile and handed the picture to him, "Can you take this, I can't destroy it."

"Sure," he smiled and took the picture away from her quivering hand. "You know, he wanted this for you from the first time you met. He wanted to give you a whole new life."

"But I bet he banked on sharing it with me."

"I suppose," he sighed and walked across the room. "But he also knew the risks, don't ever forget that.

He put you in danger." She nodded as he left the room. He was right of course, Ben was the reason she now had no one, the reason she was in America instead of being with her family. Ben had a lot to answer for.

He took it into the bathroom and tore the picture to shreds. It upset him too, he was a very good friend and found it hard to grasp that he'd never see him again. At the same time he was pissed off with him, he should have planned a better escape, he should have had a back-up plan to make sure both of them got away safely.

When he returned to the living room, the new Holly was having pictures taken. Mark decided to make a few scenic prints, to give her some history. Using different back drops and getting her to change her outfit a few times. He turned to Rory and smiled,

"What is your new name?"

"Ethan."

"Cool, you're next, Ethan, go and get a couple of different shirts, it might be a good idea to take pictures of you both together, just in case anyone asks," Ethan nodded and hurried to his room. Holding his shirts in his hands he watched as the flash went off over a hundred times, Mark turned and smiled at him, it was now his turn. No going back, Rory was gone now and Ethan was born.

Alex left with their pictures after he had made the new Ethan look like a model or a famous movie star, new hairstyle, nice clothes and sunglasses. He promised that they would have everything they needed the following afternoon.

Mark entered the living room again, his Rolex rolled on his wrist and his white shirt hung loosely over the waistband of his khaki shorts.

"Are you sure you don't mind us being here?" Holly asked.

"Of course not, in fact, I am actually enjoying it," Mark replied sincerely. "So, how about we go to the mall and get you two some new clothes to go with your new lives, all of your British stuff will be burned I'm afraid."

"Great," Ethan sighed wryly, "shopping, not a favourite of mine."

"Well, don't you want a movie star wardrobe to go with that movie star name?" Mark smiled lifting his wallet and sun glasses off the glass coffee table.

"When you put it like that," he returned the smile.

"One more thing, you both need to work on your accents, lose the Irish and English, so we only speak American."

"Hey, just remember, Mark," Ethan pointed out, "you speak our language with a horrible accent."

"I can't do southern," Holly grimaced.

"Of course you can, just add Darlin' to everything, and that you are fixin' to go somewhere, you'll get the hang of it," Mark joked as they left the penthouse.

# Five

ʊʊʊ

"And you're telling me this because?" Jock snapped at Mason.

"We don't know where she is, Gov., that's all," he explained anxiously.

"No!" Jock screamed back, his face reddened with shear infuriation, "You don't tell me she has disappeared, she canny disappear," he roared. "Is she Houdini?"

"No," Mason frowned.

"So, she can't just disappear, no one can. Go back to her family, ask them where she is; she might have let something slip." He looked at Vic, "Don't fuck this up, I will make sure you both have enough to retire out of this, if you don't fuck it up," he began to foam at the sides of his mouth out of pure rage.

"Sure," Mason nodded and they left.

"Her grandmother seemed to know more," Vic sighed as they left, "Think the old girl was holding out on us?"

"You heard him, despite the fact that you called him a stupid Scots twat, he is still prepared to pay you too."

"Fine, we'll find her, but I am not killing her, we'll get the stones and bring them back, but she goes free, you understand? That bloody maniac will rip her to pieces and she don't deserve that."

"No, of course she doesn't, if she gives us the stones, she can go," Mason agreed as they climbed into the car.

They filled their car up with unleaded, grabbed two packs of sandwiches and hit the M3 heading back to Bournemouth. Vic wasn't pleased he had to lie to his wife again, but she'd never agree to him going after this young girl. Something told him though that she knew where they were and that the decoy as clever as it was may have been her idea. She wasn't stupid and he admired the balls she had. He did not want to harm her though and he would make sure no one else would either. Would she have continued into Spain or would she be somewhere else? Mason's phone rang,

"Yeah," he groaned as he had drifted off to sleep as soon as they hit the motorway.

"It's Jock, I have my nephew here and he has a little information about this Lisa girl. Apparently she told a friend she would be going over three thousand miles away. Now I am no expert but I know Spain is a lot nearer than that. He's hacked into the flights leaving Jersey that afternoon; she hopped a flight to Dublin."

"Dublin," Mason frowned.

"I ain't goin to bloody Dublin, I hate the Irish," Vic moaned.

"For God sake, shut Tinkerbell up, will you?" Jock snapped. Vic heard every word. "She ain't going to be in Dublin, but it is a gateway to the US of A, isn't it?"

"So, you think she's State side?" Mason frowned.

"Not America, I hate the Yanks more than the Irish. Jesus Christ," Vic moaned again.

"Tell him if he's too old to go, I can always send one of my lads."

"No, that won't be necessary." He looked over at Vic, he had sped up and Mason knew he'd get a speeding ticket if he didn't watch out. "Any ideas as to where we start?" he asked.

"Not yet, just get your arses back here."

"So, we ain't gotta go down South then?"

"Correct, see you soon." Jock then hung up the phone.

"What do I tell 'er in doors, she ain't gonna buy no fishing weekend crap if we have to go traipsing around all over America." Vic groaned.

"When are you going to Spain?"

"Next week," he sighed then he smiled, "Ah, so I can tell her that I have a business trip and she will have to go without me." He liked the sound of that.

"You just need to show her who has the dick in your marriage sometimes, me old son." Mason shook his head.

"Like Monica lets you, yeah right, mate, she has a bigger dick than you and you know it," Vic chuckled.

"Yeah, well if Sheila gets wind of this you won't have a dick to talk about, will you?" Mason laughed, he was right too. Sheila would hang Vic's balls out to dry if she found out that he was still working as a heavy. She was under the impression that he was working at the boxing gym for an old friend, so she would go ballistic if she found the truth out.

When they reached Jock's office again, his genius nephew Julian was sat gleaming at them. Vic disliked him more than the Irish, more than the Yanks and much more than his uncle. He couldn't tell you why he hated the little runt so much, he just did. With his red curly hair and dusty green eyes, small face, just like a rat, he had a pointed chin and wore small, metal framed glasses, he turned Vic's stomach. But the kid was clever and they did need his help.

Vic knew him from when he used to go about with his son Steven, and he didn't like him then, he was a crack head and there is only one thing he hates more than the Jocks, the Irish and the Yanks, and that's junkies.

"Hello, Victor," he smiled arrogantly.

"Julian," Vic groaned and sat on the seat at the side of the room.

"So, are we all ready for a trip to the U S of A?" Julian asked.

"What?" Vic sat forward and looked at Mason.

"I thought we'd go on our own, Jock," Mason frowned.

"Yeah, well, you know what thought did, don't you? Thought you farted and found out you shit yourself, eh, laddie? No, I want Julian to go and make sure you two deliver this time. I want my stones and I want that little bitch to bleed for what she did," Jock snarled.

"Hang on a minute, mate," Vic stood, "we were never in this to make anyone bleed, chances are Ben copped it after your twats beat the shit out of him. I am not going to hurt the girl, she's just a kid, Jock, we hurt her, we could do bird in the States for that, I ain't about to do bird for you or anyone else."

"Alright, I'll just send my two..." Jock began, Mason cut him off.

"Look, Jock, Vic's right, we already have Ben's blood on our hands, those Yanks don't take too kindly to murderers over there, especially ones from across the pond." He looked at Vic, "We will go and we will bring her back, what you do to her will be on your head. Take it or leave it. And by the way, your twats won't get in with their records, no one gets in with a criminal record, even we have other names to travel under. I don't expect you have new passports for them, do ya?" Jock looked at Julian. "We'll take this little shit though, but he had better behave and if he touches any of that junk he's on, he's on his own," he smiled at Julian, "cos if they catch him smugglin' in shit, they will have a nice little boyfriend waiting for his arsehole to make him their bitch."

"You had better make sure he is good then, hadn't you? My sister would break my arm if anything happened to him." He warned.

"Funny though," Vic muttered, "she don't mind him hanging around with you."

ʊʊʊ

Holly sat in the back of Mark's white limousine with Mark and Ethan, she felt a little more confident that this could actually work. She wondered how her mum and brother were back home and of course her Nan. But she knew she could really get used to this sort of lifestyle. Being waited on and chauffeured around like a movie star. In her purse sat some of the cash that Mark had given her, she bought enough to buy both her and the new Ethan a new wardrobe of clothes. Drifting from store to store in downtown Houston actually put a smile on her face, one she didn't have to feel guilty about. She saved her tears for later when she would be alone.

As they climbed back into the car Ethan began to play with his new mobile phone and put on his new expensive sunglasses. Holly clutched to her bags suddenly feeling a little groggy and tired again.

Mark took them to Foley's, a large restaurant on the docks where he ordered lobster and champagne to celebrate the beginning of their new lives. Holly just wanted to go back to the penthouse, all she wanted was to rest and the smell of the lobster turned her stomach, so, she declined and settled for a salad. The afternoon dragged, but the champagne tasted good.

Finally, back at Mark's penthouse she kicked of her shoes and went to her room, she heard the phone ring and then someone knocked on her door.

"Holly, I need to speak to you," Mark said through the door. She opened the door, "We have a problem," he frowned and swallowed.

Panic filtered through her body, "What's happened?"

"Nothing to worry about, it's just the, uh, sale, it's kinda not going through the way we hoped." He explained cautiously.

"I don't understand," she frowned.

"In plain terms, the buyer only wants half the stones, I can find someone else for the other half, but it might take a few days."

"Mark, this is serious," she sighed feeling uneasy and sat on the bed, "what am I going to do?"

"Listen, ten million is still a lot of money, Lis... I mean, Holly. I promise you, I will do my upmost to get another buyer. I have a lot of connections, so, don't worry about it, I may push for more for you."

"Just sell them, Mark, please, I want nothing more to do with them," she grumbled.

"I know, honey, I know," he sighed. "On the up side, I have these," he handed her an envelope. "Alex got them early for you." She flicked through the papers, and looked up at him.

"So, I am now Holly, no more Lisa and no more English girl, now I am a Yank."

"Uh, we don't take too kindly to Yanks in these here parts, Miss," Mark winked his eye. "Welcome to America."

She wanted to share his joy, but she was worried, she knew she'd leave in a few days with ten million dollars' worth of diamonds, blood diamonds, and the very same stones to cause her to lose Ben.

The bank account was opened the following morning. Mark had instructed the buyers to deposit the funds of nine million dollars into her account by five that day and the stones would be couriered by two of Mark's men to LA, where they would meet up with some of the far eastern buyers.

Mark and Ethan divided the stones equally and gave half of them back to Holly; she picked out one stone and gave it to Mark.

"I don't need this," he said.

"I want you to have it," she insisted pushing his hand back, "after all you have done for us, I will never be able to thank you, Mark."

"But I owed it to Ben, you don't understand."

"I do, you took me in and you helped me, Mark. I wouldn't have known what to do, I truly wouldn't. So, please take it and I don't know make it into a ring or some earrings for your girlfriend."

"I don't have a girlfriend," he smiled, "but thank you, Holly, this is really too much."

"You're welcome," she said in a clear undisputable American accent.

"Now I am impressed," he beamed.

"What about me?" Ethan asked.

"Oh, you sound like John Wayne," Mark smiled. "I am going to miss you two."

"You can always visit," Holly smiled, "it is your house after all."

"That is true," he replied, gazing into her eyes. "Well, I had better get these ready, I have to get my boys ready. I need these to be on the road in an hour." He explained and left the room.

"That was a five carat gem you gave him, Holly," Ethan frowned.

"We have plenty," she smiled, "I like him, he has been so nice."

"He has, it's your gig and it's good to have someone we can trust with us," he added. "So, when do we leave?"

"I think we should go tomorrow," she replied and placed the stones inside her purse. "I'll need to find somewhere to store them."

He nodded, "Yeah, it's not safe to keep them in your bag," Ethan pointed out obviously.

ᘘᘘᘘ

Their flight had already been delayed by two hours, Mason sat watching the world go by in the departure lounge, and Vic sat watching Julian play solitaire on his lap top. He had no idea how to use one, but seemed quite happy to watch someone else on one. Vic was no Techno head, he hated all gadgets and their many forms. When Steven asked for an iPod for Christmas he thought he meant some sort of tent or a new fishing rod, he didn't know you could store up to five thousand songs on one. Why would he? If the TV played up he'd give Sheila the money to get a new one, whether they needed to replace it or not. He wasn't rich, but he would rather buy a new one then pay someone to fix it. So, he watched the music shop that didn't even sell records anymore, the huge duty free shop and a couple of children playing on some rides outside.

"How long does it take to turn a flight around?" Vic groaned.

"I'll check the boards," Julian said standing and placing his laptop on the seat.

"Well, he's behaving himself so far," Mason smiled.

"Yeah, he'd better," Vic frowned as he returned.

"We can go to the gate now," he announced lifting his computer. "Ready?"

"Yeah," Mason stood. The seat had all but welded itself to his backside and it felt numb.

Vic insisted on the window seat and Mason did not want to be stuck in the middle but felt sure that Julian might cop it if he didn't, so he sat next to Vic and smiled at the cabin crew as they passed.

"Too young for ya, mate," Vic nudged him.

"I can dream," Mason grinned.

Before they took off Vic was snoring making Mason wish he'd found a seat somewhere else, his heavy breathing was going to make this a long flight. Once they were airborne the stewardess came with drinks and Mason elbowed Vic in the side to wake him,

"What the hell was that?" Vic moaned.

"Turbulence," Mason and Julian said together.

"Would you like something to drink, sir?" the pretty blonde asked.

"Uh, I'll have a beer please, love," Mason smiled.

"Make that two," Vic added.

"I'll have a J D and coke," Julian grinned.

"Do you have some I.D.?" she asked him.

"Uh, yeah," Julian nodded and handed her his passport.

"I'm sorry, sir, as this is an American airline and you have to be twenty one to drink alcohol. I can get you the coke though," she handed him a can of coke, he looked at it and then at Vic, who was smiling from ear to ear. She then left after giving the others their beers.

"Looks like you'll be in for a long flight," Vic chuckled.

"Shut up," Julian snapped and reclined his seat back. Mason cracked his can over Julian,

"Mmm," he teased, "that tastes good."

Julian closed his eyes and tried to sleep, he didn't want to show them how annoyed he was.

ᚥᚥᚥ

"This place is going to get quiet," Mark sighed as he hugged Ethan goodbye. "I would come with you, but I am needed here at the moment," he handed her a list of numbers. "You have my cell and my work number there, if you need anything just call. I had my housekeeper stock up, so you'll have all you need and I will try and get down this weekend, okay?"

"Sure, uh, thanks for everything, Mark," Holly smiled and hugged him.

"It's been a pleasure meeting you, I just hope your life is as exciting and as happy as you deserve," she smiled again and climbed into the hire car beside Ethan.

Lisa and Rory were gone forever and the future as uncertain as it seemed, could only get better.

# Six

She gazed back at Houston where the city seemed to drop into the ocean as they headed north. The road seemed to wind on and on and the music on the radio made her miss home. The heat was reflecting off the road, heat ripples danced like liquid in front of them and air con drained at the fuel, but they couldn't drive without it. At the second stop for gas, she tried out her all new American accent on the cashier.

"Hey," the small, red-haired girl smiled as she approached the counter.

"Hey," Holly replied coolly.

"So, where ya headed?" she asked as she rang up the drinks in the cash register.

"Oh, we're just passing through," she smiled, "not sure where to stop for the night actually."

"Long journey, huh?"

"You could say that," Holly smiled again, "Anywhere we would need to avoid?"

"Depends on how much farther you have to go?"

"We're heading towards Austin, my brother wants to check out the school there," she lied.

"Oh, well then, unless you are real tired, you could make it by eleven tonight, there are a few motels on the way if you'd prefer."

"No, we'll just keep going then I suppose," she shrugged.

"Is that a New England accent?" she asked.

"Yeah," Holly admitted, "is it that obvious?"

"It's definitely not Texan," the cashier called Emily grinned again. "Have a safe trip," she handed Holly the receipt and watched as she left. She said thanks and hurried out into the warm afternoon air, Ethan was leaning against the car.

"I'll drive now," she said climbing back into the car, Ethan yawned and stretched before climbing in the passenger side. "I have this accent almost whipped," she beamed complacently.

"I noticed," he smiled and snapped his seatbelt in. "You do know we drive on the other side of the road over here."

"Ha, ha, very funny," she giggled and drove back out onto the highway.

The violet sky darkened as they drove the dark purple roads with only their headlights in front of them. Holly found a radio station she actually liked, playing nineties songs reminding her of her childhood and the fun she had dancing around her bedroom singing to *Take That* and the *Spice Girls.*

Ethan had fallen asleep not long after they got back onto the main highway. So she hummed to the music and tapped her thumbs on the steering wheel along with the beat, anything to keep her awake.

When she hit the Austin city limits, she woke Ethan so he could read out the directions to Mark's private little Idaho. They followed the map and drove out of the other side of the city,

"Are you sure this is the right way?" she asked.

"Yes, we are following them word for word," he grimaced, impatiently. "I am bursting for a pee," he groaned. She gazed over and stopped the car. "I am not getting out here."

"Well, you need a pee, get out and pee," she snapped.

"Fine," he opened the door and climbed out into the warm and humid night air. The crickets chirped loudly, like singing birds as he gazed around to ensure he was not about to get attacked by a wolf or a bear. When he was finished, he realised he had just peed over a gate post. When he looked more closely, he could see it was to a huge house that sat back in the trees. He raced back to the car and lifted the paper from his seat. "We're here, I thought he said a little house," he added with a frown, she looked over at where Ethan was pointing. "That's a mansion."

"Great, so much for a little hideaway," she sighed and started the engine to the car again.

When they got inside the house was even bigger, she gazed around at the cream painted walls and the huge windows with white venetian blinds. The house was completely open inside, no walls to separate the living room from the dining room or kitchen. The large stair case wound up to a huge landing, carpeted in white and spotlessly clean. She gazed at Ethan who was as much in awe as she was.

"Do you want something to eat?" he asked her glaring over at the kitchen area.

"No, I am too tired to eat," she frowned.

Ethan locked the front door behind them and followed her up the stairs carrying her bags for her. She opened the first door at the top of the stairs, it was a huge bathroom with a kidney shaped bath tub that looked so inviting. He smiled at her as her eyes sparkled in the lights. He then opened a door immediately to the left, it was a bedroom with a huge bed and a closet the width of the room. It had dark green walls and a large window.

"I'll take this one then," he said thinking at least he was close to the bathroom. She nodded in agreement and was almost too afraid to open the next door. She switched on the light to the room, it was decorated in a deep gold colour, with a huge white four post bed with white swags of fabric hanging down. The bed had about twenty pillows and cushions on it and the window was actually a balcony.

She opened another door and this opened into a separate bathroom, of white and silver with a black tiled floor. Another door revealed a walk in closet, she turned and smiled excitedly at Ethan,

"I'll take this one."

"Mmm, maybe I should, I mean…"

"No, you keep that other one, maybe you won't make so much mess."

"I'm not messy," he protested.

"I have been to your flat, remember?"

"I thought you were too upset to notice," he admitted, pain graced her face, "sorry, I am an asshole."

"It's fine," she swallowed.

"So, you get this room with your own bathroom."

"Yes," she gazed around, "I'll need a lot more clothes to fill that closet though."

"I am sure there's a mall around here somewhere," he smiled. "So, is everything to your liking, Ma'am?" she nodded and smiled, "In that case, I am going to bed, goodnight, Holly."

"Good night, Ethan," she smiled again.

She didn't think about how comfortable and soft the bed was or how good the clean sheets felt, crisp and fresh against her tired body, or the fact that the down quilt wrapped around her the way Ben used to. No, her mind was blank, her eyes closed and she drifted off to sleep and back into his arms. Yes this certainly wasn't the life she had planned on, but put Mark into the mix, she could cope; she truly believed she would get through this and get herself a happy ever after.

ღღღ

"How long are you staying then, sir?" the young looking immigration officer asked as Mason tried to keep his cool.

"To be honest, mate, I am visiting an old flame and you know how things can go, so, I might be here a week or four, that's why I got an open ticket."

"But you understand you can't stay any longer than three months without a visa?"

"Of course I do, look I can't be here that long anyway, I have a job to get back to, you know."

"Good, well enjoy your stay, Mr Fagin, I hope you enjoy Boston."

"Thanks, mate," Mason smiled and collected his passport and papers.

"Mr Sykes," the pretty, green eyed immigration officer smiled, "Welcome to America, is this your first trip?" she asked.

"Yes, I am helping my mate find his first girlfriend." He lied.

"Oh, how sweet," she grinned. "I have always wanted to go to England."

"You should, we can always use more pretty ladies like yourself."

"Well, thank you," she blushed slightly. "Enjoy your stay," she handed him his stamped passport with another friendly smile.

They met up with Julian and headed towards the Dollar rental to collect their car. Pushing their bags on a luggage cart, Julian couldn't help but chuckle.

"Sikes and Fagin," he snickered as they waited for their car, "couldn't you two come up with a better name than to pinch them off a bloody film."

"Nope, what about you, who is it you have called yourself again?" Vic snarled.

"William Thatcher," Mason smiled, "either you're related to old Maggie or you got that from that film with the Knights in it."

"A Knights Tale," he sighed, "okay, I'll shut up."

"Good idea," Vic grinned. He was tired and hungry and the car was taking too long for him.

The roar of a jet engine echoed out as they waited in the garage for their hire car. It was Vic's first time in New England, he had been to Florida with the kids and to Vegas with Mason a long time ago, but this part of the States had never been relevant to his life. As he hated the Yanks, he thought it best to stay out of their country.

Finally, a small red Chevy stopped in front of them. Vic looked at Mason slightly miffed.

"It's Jock's idea, less conspicuous." Mason shrugged.

"You don't say," Vic moaned and lifted the trunk. "This boot is too small for this Muppet to sleep in," he smiled at Julian.

"Oh you're a laugh a minute ain't ya?" Julian replied, "I am gonna re name you two Little and Large," he chuckled and climbed into the back of the car, "Bloody comedians, the pair of ya."

"Little and bloody Large, cheeky sod," Vic frowned. "Right then first stop is a hotel," Vic yawned, "I need to get me head down."

"I could eat a horse," Mason said climbing into the car. "Let's get some grub first, then we can find a hotel."

"Yeah, well, beauty does need his sleep," Julian agreed. Vic was far too tired to even retaliate, plus he was bored of this kid and wondered how long it would take them to track Lisa down.

# Seven

When she opened her eyes to the sunlit room, she caught the mouth-watering aroma of cooked bacon. She pushed back the soft white covers and stood from the bed, she still feeling tired and lethargic, but at least she could get on with her life now, that was all the motivation she needed at that point. She had dreamed of Ben and ached to be with him again. But she couldn't and had to accept that, time stopped for no one, she had to move forward.

She could hear Ethan down stairs, so she found a robe that belonged to Mark hanging on the back of the bathroom door and headed down the winding staircase to the kitchen. U2 were singing 'One' and Ethan. in fine Irish tongue, sang along with it. She smiled as she sat at the tabled and poured herself a glass of orange juice. He turned and flashed an embarrassed smile.

"Top of the morning to ya," he grinned.

"We're meant to be American," she groaned.

"I know," he shrugged his shoulders and placed a plate of bacon and eggs in front of her. "So, what are we going to do today?"

"Thanks, I don't know," she sighed. "You don't have to cook for me."

"Well, I was making some anyway. I was thinking that I might go to college, get Mark to fake some school papers and get a business degree or something," he continued as he sat opposite her.

"You could, but how long are we staying here? I mean, Mark has been really good Ethan, but I don't want to take advantage of him."

"Yes, but he did say we could stay as long as we needed, and Austin is a big city, you could really lose yourself here."

"True," she lifted her fork thinking about his words. "I promised to pay you a million and that still stands, there is nothing to say that you have to stay with me permanently. You can go off to college or disappear in Alaska if that is what you want to do."

"I know, but I like being around you, you seem so…sad and lonely Lis…I mean, Holly."

"I'll be alright; I can't rely on you now, can I?" she asked.

"I don't see why not," he sipped his juice, "right now though, we need some wheels and somewhere else to live. I am going to enjoy my new life," he was right, she did still need to have him around and knew she'd never get through the next few weeks alone. Ben had been dead a week and her life had changed so much. She owed it to him to make it.

Over the next couple of days they shopped and found two cars that they both liked, hers was an Audi sports car, silver with white leather seats and Ethan found a huge BMW X5 in black, both were second hand as they didn't want to give the locals the wrong impression.

They spoke to one of the realtors in town and they said they would keep an eye out for the perfect house for them. She told Mark that they planned to stay in Austin and he agreed it would be a good idea. She had given Ethan his money and he opened himself a bank account. Mark's lawyer friend sent the school transcripts to prove Ethan had been in school and had aced his exams.

They told anyone they met they were brother and sister and no one seemed to have a reason not to believe them. Holly went with Ethan when he signed up at the University of Texas and they bought Longhorns shirts to celebrate his acceptance. They kept a reasonably low profile and never dined out or anything. But the walls were closing in and with Ethan ready to start school in the next few days, Holly knew she'd need something to occupy her mind.

Mark drove down alone to visit them as promised and was amazed at how settled they both were. He took them out to dinner at his country club to celebrate. Holly wore a dark blue dress and pinned the sides of her hair up and Ethan showed off his new Levis and gold belt buckle.

"You wouldn't know that you were from up yonder," Mark grinned and sipped his wine.

"No," Holly shook her head, "we are doing our best to blend."

"It's working," he smiled admiringly. Ethan glared around the room and caught the eye of a pretty waitress. "One thing you need to learn though, my friend, we don't date the help."

"I don't want to date her," Ethan smiled; "I just want to shag her." Holly drew in a deep breath and rolled her eyes, Mark beckoned Ethan towards him and he leaned in close.

"We don't say *shag* over here, *mate*," Mark said as he winked his eye. "Plus, she is the easiest chic here. Stay away from those college girls too, you could get drunk, tell them one thing and by tomorrow the whole campus would know everything. Just keep doing what you are doing and in a few months you can think about girls, okay, buddy?"

"A few months," Ethan frowned and looked at Holly, instantly feeling bad, "Sorry, Holly," he said leaning back towards his seat. She smiled sweetly and shrugged,

"You can do what you like, Ethan," she said and sipped her wine, Ethan had his own life to lead,

"I know, but..." he looked at Mark, he needed to change the subject, "What do you think of my wheels?"

"Sweet, man," Mark smiled approvingly, "I never had you pegged to buy a sports car, Holly."

"I have always wanted an Audi," she explained.

"I like Porsches myself, but you have to have something with a little meat on the bones in Texas." He grinned.

"I see you bought your big ol' truck down, Mark," Ethan smiled.

"Yeah, she's my lady, reminds me of my mother actually."

"What, you mean, big and noisy?"

"No, reliable, comfortable and pretty to look at," he smiled.


Once back at the house, Mark announced he was leaving the following morning, but wanted to show Holly the safety deposit vault before he left. She went to bed early and feeling bad as she knew she was in his room and he had to take the guest room down stairs. This made her decide that they had to look for their own house, whether Ethan wanted to move in with her or not. So, after the safety deposit, she was heading to the relaters to see what she could buy.

Before she went to bed they sat on the couch in the huge living room. "You're quiet, Holly, are you okay?" Mark asked her.

"I'm a little off today, I didn't sleep very well last night," she explained.

"No, I guess it's all still a bit wild for you," he frowned slightly.

"Actually, I am bored silly, I need to find a job, Mark."

"Well, what did you do before you came here?"

"I worked for a small office, we made credit cards," she loved her job and missed everyone there.

"Cool," he nodded, "you don't need the money, but I can see how you might be feeling bored. I am sure there's something here and I'll have Jay, my assistant, write you a reference."

"Thanks, Mark, again," she smiled.

"Anything I can do to help," he also smiled.

ᛒᛒᛒ

The motel sat on the edge of the main interstate through Boston. The room was clean if nothing else, there were two huge beds, but both Vic and Mason decided that Julian could have the couch. There was also a small table and a TV on the wall. He sat eating from a huge bag of crisps while tapping away on his laptop. The cars and trucks roared by outside and as Vic lay on the bed to try and sleep, Mason switched on the TV. Vic tossed and turned, but in the end he had to say something,

"It's like trying to sleep at Clapham Junction in here, you with your bloody tap, tap, tapin' on that thing and you with the whiney American soaps, how is anyone meant to get some kip?"

"Victor, if you sleep now you won't sleep tonight," Julian replied smartly.

"I am going to ram that thing down your fuckin' throat if you don't pack it in, I am warning you, sunshine," Vic snarled. "Call me Victor again and the only way you are going to be able to Google is up your bloody arse, got it?"

"Got it, Vic," Julian saluted him. Mason smiled; he loved seeing Vic get so wound up by this kid. "I am only trying to stop you getting jet lagged."

"It ain't jetlag, you twat. I am just tired, since I started on this gig, I ain't had a nights kip, so all I want is forty winks, now fuckin' shut up."

"Vic, you really need to calm down, me old mate, that language is appallin'," Mason said as he switched off the TV.

"Yeah, you shut up too," Vic snapped. Mason rolled his eyes and opened the door.

"I am going to see if I can find some beer, I need a drink."

"What if my uncle calls?" Julian asked.

"Take a message," Mason answered.

"I am not here to be your fuckin' secretary," Julian snapped angrily.

"Why not, you look like her, in fact, you have about the same amount of facial hair as she does too," Mason smiled. "Get the kettle on, love, and make Vic a cuppa." He then shut the door behind him; Vic turned over and buried his ears in his pillows.

ᗡᗡᗡ

Mark left after showing Holly the safety deposit boxes at the back of the bank. He used them and even the staff knew him by his first name, which was reassuring to Holly. She locked the diamonds away and took the key out to the assistant as she waited by the vault door.

Mark dropped her off before leaving and she felt slightly sad to see him leave. Alone and bored she decided to go into town that afternoon and have a look around. She had been seen a lot with Ethan and thought that when his classes started she'd have to get used to being alone sometime.

The streets of Austin city centre were so clean; the only place she had seen cleaner was Berlin. She and Ben had gone for a weekend trip and they loved it. But the memories made her miss him more, she shook it off and proceeded to visit the many stores that lined the streets. She found a cute candle shop and went inside to find some for the house. Mark had said they could stay as long as they needed and with the realtors looking for the perfect house for them, she had no idea how long it would take. So an open invitation was most welcome.

Holly enjoyed Mark's company, one reason was because it made her feel close to Ben and the other was that he seemed so together, so calm about everything. She felt as though her life was crumbling away and he showed her how to dust herself off and appear to be stronger even if she wasn't, even if she was so home sick, she cried herself to sleep every night.

After finding two of the best smelling vanilla candles in the store, she found a small coffee shop just up the street and sat in the sun waiting for her latte to be bought out to her. The birds sung in the trees as she began to wonder if all was okay at home, if Jock had hurt her family, the fear of that caused her pain and almost crushed her, but she knew it could be true.

She pulled it all back in and watched the cars as they passed by and at shoppers busying the streets, some with children in and others were happy couples. Holding hands, meandering down the street, happy.

"That's the worst thing you can do," someone said, she turned her head to see a man with light blond hair and bright blue eyes.

"Excuse me?" she said perfectly American.

"Uh, look at happy couples when you are so alone." He elaborated.

"How do you know I am alone?" she asked.

"Uh," he pointed to her ring finger, "me too," he cracked an amazing, lopsided smile. His accent was strong and southern; his teeth were as white as snow.

"Well, I have just got out of something sticky, so…"

"Me too," he smiled again as he stood. "I'll let you enjoy your coffee in peace," he said.

"Thank you," she swallowed.

"Take care now," he called back as he walked down the street.

At least if she had Ethan with her, she was left alone, so others thinking that they were a couple would stop all the men looking for one thing. How could she ever trust anyone? Would they be legitimate or were they just after the diamonds? She couldn't allow herself to trust a soul, let alone a perfect stranger even if he was good looking and a gentleman.

On her way back to the car her cell rang, it was Ethan and whenever he called she panicked.

"Hello?" she frowned.

"Hey, uh, where are you?"

"In town, I am just about to head home," she replied.

"The realtors have called, they found us a house, do you want to meet me there?"

"Okay," she beamed an excited grin, suddenly feeling a little better and the panic was over.

# Eight

She followed his directions and found the house that backed on to some woods and the nearest neighbour was about a mile away. It was two story and painted white stone. The red brick drive way was big and the house was surrounded in trees. Hidden away from the main road and a little bit off the beaten track, but she fell in love with it immediately. The emerald lawn hissed with the sprinklers and the shady trees rustled in the afternoon breeze.

"Hi, I am Carol Lane," a small blonde with a huge smile and brown eyes said as she approached Holly.

"Holly Long."

"Yes, uh, your brother is on his way, so, shall we make a start?" Holly nodded her head and followed her inside the house, not that she needed to see it, this house was perfect and nothing could put her off.

Inside, a huge staircase ran up in front of them, the banister was dark wood to match the floors of the down stairs. She followed Carol from room to room and fell deeper for this home, it felt like a home should feel, inviting and cosy. Upstairs she showed Holly the main bedroom with adjoining bathroom and then the other three bedrooms, it seemed huge but she planned on being there the rest of her life.

All of the walls were in pastel colours with huge closets. There were two other bathrooms on that floor and in the attic they discovered another room. Out of the window you could see out into the open fields. Holly smiled as she followed Carol back down the stairs she could really picture herself living there. Even with Ethan at college she felt comfortable and safe for the first time since she had left home.

The kitchen seemed huge, even compared to Mark's though similar, except it was dark wood with terracotta painted walls and small mosaic tiles surrounding the cooker and sink area.

"The kitchen will come with the stove, dishwasher and refrigerator." Carol explained. "Of course the laundry is also fully fitted out."

"Hello?" Ethan called out walking through the house, he found the girls in the kitchen. "This is great, right, sis?" he asked.

"Yes, actually, uh, where do I sign?" Holly nodded.

"You want to…sign?" Carol smiled excitedly.

"Yes, I love it, so, when can we move in?"

"You haven't even asked me the price," Carol queried.

"I will pay the asking price, I am desperate to have my own house and we really need to move soon. I can't be bothered with haggling over a few dollars," Holly explained.

"Well, I will get the papers drawn up and we can get the ball rolling," Carol gleamed with excitement, it must have meant a lot to her to sell this house. "Oh, did you want to see the pool? There's a pool house, you know, for when you have family come and visit." Family, they had no family, it was just them. Before she could wallow further, Ethan snapped her back.

"Great," he beamed; "is it through there?" he asked as he pointed to a door.

"No, that's the garage, the previous owner liked to keep private, there are some extra rooms off the garage, he kept them in case we were invaded," she smiled, "you know, being so close to Roswell and all."

"Aliens, cool," Ethan grinned.

"Now you have started him off," Holly chuckled.

ᚹᚹᚹ

"No, Jock, we haven't had so much as a peep out of her," Mason rolled his tired eyes, three days they had been stuck in a motel room listening to the traffic pass outside.

"Listen, Sonny Jim, I am getting pissed off with all this waiting around. Where could that little bitch be?"

"I wish I knew," Mason sighed. "Look, I am confident she might have met someone here, an American or Irish. Maybe we should hit some bars, see if any of them know anything about and English girl or possibly Irish girl coming here." He suggested.

"Just do anything," Jock shouted. It woke Julian who had dosed off through pure boredom. Mason hung up the phone he then announced,

"It looks like we are going out tonight."

"Great, just what I always wanted, a night out in an American bar, drinking piss week beer and watching the 'game' on telly," Vic groaned.

"Can't you do anything without fuckin' moaning, Vic?" Julian asked as he stood from the chair.

"Well, you can't come with us can you, no one can get served with alcoholic drinks under twenty one here, remember?" Vic smiled. "So that's a plus, I would say."

"Ha, ha bloody ha," Julian snapped and went to the bathroom.

"Is there any building sites near here?" Vic asked.

"No," Mason frowned.

"Shame, I could just give 'Clever Dick' a pair of concrete boots and throw him in the bloody drink," Vic smiled.

"And what would you say to Jock?"

"I dunno, sharks got him or something," he smirked.

"That sea is the Atlantic, Vic, I am bloody positive that sharks don't like that one."

Vic snickered, "Mason, I do believe you have lost your sense of humour."

"Yeah, it's bein' around you twenty-four-seven, you are turning into Alf Garnet, mate." Mason smiled.

After a long shower and a shave, including his head, Vic was ready to leave. Mason bought in some beer so Julian could have a drink, he sat working on his laptop and Vic cracked one more joke before he left,

"Bo peep by seven, now, there's a good lad."

"Up yours you old bastard," Julian snapped.

It had rained outside and smelled fresher as they crossed the street to try and get a taxi back into the city. The motel receptionist recommended a couple of bars in the Harvard area, but neither of them fancied a night of college kids and decided to go towards the city centre.

The bar wasn't as big as it looked from outside, they went to the bar and ordered two beers. Vic glanced around and realised something very quickly, there weren't any women in the bar and then the barman winked as he put to bottles of Budweiser on the bar.

"I do not believe this," Vic moaned lowering his head.

"What now?" Mason sighed.

"All I am saying is, if you drop something, do not bend over to pick it up, 'cos if you do, you are on your own."

"What the…" Mason looked around and the barman smiled raising his eyebrows. "Uh, right then, mate, time to go," he placed ten dollars on the counter and they headed for the door watched by all. Once outside they both breathed a sigh of relief.

"Never, in all my natural 'ave I ever been in a bloody gay's pub and now, 'cos of this gig I 'ave. You tell anyone, Mason and I will…" he warned.

"I know, you think I want that lot at the King to know, course not," he smiled, and then began to chuckle. "Fuckin' funny though, mate, I 'ave to give you that," he laughed louder. "Don't bend over, lucky you said that, there were a couple of coins on the floor and I needed a Gypsy's." They both laughed hard together and Vic remembered the fun they had when they were younger, before the life of crime and violence.

They headed further down the street and found another bar, luckily though this had drinkers of both sexes and Vic was relieved to finally be able to enjoy a beer.

"Get many Paddy's in here?" Mason asked the barman.

"I beg your pardon," the barman frowned.

"Oh, uh, Irish, do they come in here much?"

"Only on Celts nights," he replied placing a glass of iced, cold beer in front of Vic.

"Celtic, but there a Scottish football club," Vic frowned.

"The Boston Celtics, sir, they play basketball at the Fleet centre. You could try the bars by there, if you are looking for some Irish, there are a lot around that area." He answered placing a second beer in front of Mason.

"Cheers, mate," Mason nodded and turned to Vic. "Scottish football club, you plank." He sipped his beer and almost coughed it out when he saw the funny side of it.

"You know, it's customary to leave a tip for the barman here," a small, red haired girl smiled.

"Is that right?" Mason grinned and turned back to the barman, he beckoned him closer, "I got a tip for ya, mate, stay away from that Bahama's bar down the road, it's a gay bar," he tapped him twice on the shoulder and smiled.

"She means you give him some money," Vic chuckled, "and you called me a plank."

ᙡᙡᙡ

Back at Mark's house, Carol, the real estate woman, placed a pile of papers in front of Holly; she smiled and sifted through them, not really understanding them, Carol assured her that they were all perfectly legal. So she just skipped to the back and almost signed them as Lisa, stopped herself and signed Holly Long.

She had already arranged for the transfer of three hundred and fifty thousand dollars to be paid into the Estate agents bank account and Carol handed her the keys. Now all they had to do was furnish it. She was so excited she called Mark first,

"Hello, Mark Hobbs," he said.

"Hey, it's uh, Holly."

"Hello, Holly what are ya doing?"

"I just bought a house."

"What?" he sat up in his seat, shocked by what she had said, but pleased to hear her voice.

"I said, I bought a house," she repeated.

"So, you're staying in Austin?" he smiled.

"Yes, I like it here," she replied.

"And you have that accent, you are doing it girl, you are living the dream."

"Well, I was bursting to tell someone," she beamed, "so, you got back okay then?"

"Yes, I did. When are you moving in?"

"I don't know, I have to buy furniture and stuff so, start from scratch really," she explained.

"In my garage, there's a sofa and a dining room suite if you want it, I was going to give it to Good Will, but you can have it to make a start if you like."

"Are you sure?" she smiled.

"Of course I am. I need to get back to work, say Hi to Ethan for me."

"I will, hey, maybe when I have moved in, you will let me cook for you or something."

"I would like that a lot," he smiled again.

They said goodbye and she called Ethan to tell him the good news.

That afternoon she sat at Mark's computer and looked at some on line furniture stores. She used her shiny new gold card and ordered whatever caught her eyes. A huge solid oak coffee table and some beds, she enjoyed herself until her stomach turned and she felt sick again. She barely made it to the bathroom before throwing up in the toilet.

It was becoming a regular thing in the afternoons, either she would throw up or feel as if she would. She had never slept so much in her life before either. Then she had to think, these symptoms were either a bug or something else and the something else scared her more than anything. She remembered Marnie at her old job, she had similar symptoms and the results that followed, she glared at her reflection, this had to be a bug.

She hadn't thought about it, but her last period was weeks and weeks ago, before she and Ben left London, weeks before that even. But it could only be a bug; there was no way life would be that cruel as to make her face something she had never even dreamed before, alone.

After rinsing her mouth she headed to the nearest drugstore and bought a test.

"That works best in the morning, honey," the elderly sales assistant smiled.

"Do you have one that's for any time?" she asked.

"Sure, is it your first?" she asked walking towards the huge line of testing kits.

"Yes. Actually, I'm new in town, where would be the best doctor's surgery around?"

"Uh, oh, you mean doctor's office, are you from up north?"

"That's right," she smiled and swallowed.

"Yes, I could tell by your accent, Mass I'd say?"

"Yeah," she smiled, "you are good at accents."

"Thank you." She smiled and handed her a piece of paper. "This is the best one; it can be done anytime of the day and as early as a week late."

"Thanks."

"I'll right down the number for Dr Munroe's office, she is real sweet and she'll help you anyway you need."

"You have been very kind, thank you." Holly said and paid for the test.

"Don't mention it," she replied and gave her the change.

When Holly got back to the house Ethan was home,

"Where were you?" he asked. "I was worried."

"I had to get something, the house is paid for and I have started getting stuff for it," she said running up the stairs to her room. "I'll be right back."

She read the instructions through twice, and peed on the stick. Then she had to wait three minutes, a plus sign was positive.

All of a sudden there it was, she burst into tears, how could this be, why would he do this to her? Wasn't it enough that he took her Ben away? Now she would be a mother at twenty two, how could she cope with a child alone in another country, away from her family doctor, her mum?

"Holly, are you alright?" Ethan called through the door.

"Uh, yes, I uh, I'm just coming." She washed her face and hid the evidence in her rubbish bin.

"What is it?" he asked as she came out and sat on the bed.

"I thought it was stress, you know, with all that has happened to me over the past few weeks or so. I have been tired and irritable, and recently I have been throwing my guts up every day."

"Oh no, Holly, you're not, are you?" Ethan sighed as he sat beside her.

"I don't know what to do," she began to cry, he rested his arm across her shoulder.

"It's all right, we'll deal with it."

"What?" she asked, wiping her face on her arm.

"Well, if you want I am sure we can find someone to take care of it."

"Take care of *it*," she pushed off his arm and stood, "so, you mean get rid of it?"

"A baby would complicate things," he reasoned.

"You don't think I know that. This is Ben's baby, Ethan. I can't just get bloody rid of it," she snapped dropping her accent for the first time since she started using it.

"Okay, sorry for even suggesting it. I thought that's what you wanted."

"I don't know what I want," she sniffed and wiped her eyes, "sorry."

"I'll go and make you some tea, I found a little shop that sells Tetley, can you believe it? I bet you could murder a cup," she glared at him. "Sorry, wrong choice of words." He walked to the door. "Despite what you think, I won't leave you, Holly, and anyone else who comes along," he smiled.

"Thanks," she tried to smile.

He left her in her room and she collapsed on the bed, holding herself across the middle. She wondered when it would come, when she would be a mother. But she knew she couldn't get rid of the baby, no matter what, this baby would have a chance. Soon, she drifted off to sleep, like she did most afternoons.

Ethan made her tea and bought it up to her, but she was fast asleep, so he went downstairs and called Mark. Surely he'd be able to talk some sense into her. She liked Mark, he could tell, she would listen to Mark, she had to.

"How far along is she?" Mark asked a little disappointed.

"We don't know, she's only just done the test," Ethan explained.

"She wants to keep it?"

"She says its Ben's and she can't just get rid of it. I don't know, Mark, I think it will be a huge problem. What if we have to run, with a tiny baby that could also get killed, what then?"

"I know," he frowned, "I'm tied up in meetings until the weekend, I'll drive down then, okay?"

"Thanks, man."

"It's fine just uh, just don't push the issue, she might bolt, if you know what I mean." He warned.

"Sure thing," Ethan agreed.

# Nine

"Fleet Centre please, mate," Vic stated as he and Mason climbed into the back of a cab.

They sped through the almost deserted streets in silence. Vic was tired, when he drank beer, all he really wanted was a hot cup of tea and to go to bed, but Mason promised Jock he would do his best. It wasn't even ten and they still had a few more hours of drinking left in them.

"Hey," Vic called forward as they passed something familiar, "is that the one from that program?"

"Yeah, the Cheers bar," the cab driver replied, "that's where they all started, Ted Danson, Woody Harrelson, that's the place."

"I want to go there," Vic smiled.

"It was a damn shame when they stopped making that program, I liked it," the driver continued.

"I wished they finish bloody EastEnders," Vic added, "gives us Cockneys a bad name."

"Oh, I know EastEnders, we get it on BBC USA," the driver smiled, "the wife likes that Dot woman."

"Yeah and half of them are not even from the East end," Mason sighed. "Anyone would think we're all grimy, live in the pub and don't 'ave washing machines at home."

"We did wonder," the driver chuckled. "Here we go, are you looking for somewhere in particular?"

"Any pub that the Irish drink in," Vic said.

"Flannigan's is a good Irish bar, try there first." The cab pulled over outside a bar,

"Cheers, mate," Vic smiled handing him a twenty and told him to keep the change.

"You keep giving your money away, mate, you will be skint by the end of the week." Mason groaned as they walked towards some loud music and smashing glass.

"Irish," they said together.

Knowing his daughter was weeks away from walking up the aisle to marry one, Mason had no choice but to try and get on with them. You can't pick who your children fall in love with, but he would have given anything to make sure she didn't fall for an Irish Gypsy boxer. What can you say when you work at most of the fights he's participating in? If it weren't for that fact, she'd never have met him in the first place. So, he had to go along with it. Plus Monica couldn't wait, she loved the idea of a huge wedding, even if they had to change the venue three times, because when the organiser found out it was a Gypsy wedding, they would cancel it.

It took Vic and Mason to bribe the manager of the Allendale Hotel on the bank of the Thames to agree to have the wedding, but only then if they agreed there would be no trouble. It meant calling in a few favours from their mates who would act as door men for the day.

Vic had no idea how unhappy Mason was about the whole wedding, but you cannot choose who your children marry and both of them knew that. At least he wasn't a gangster or a drug lord; he was a short, blond,

Irish Gypsy with bright blue eyes and spoke so fast that no one could understand him half the time.

His daughter was to be known as the Gorgy Gal and that suited Charlotte fine. The other girls in the family respected her and the fact that she loved Sean, even if she wasn't a Gypsy girl or a Traveller. She knew she'd be looked after and when they moved to Ireland, they'd have a nice house big enough for when her parents came to visit, this was Sean's promise and he would never lie to her.

He had paid a lot of money towards the wedding and she loved him more than life. Obviously her parents wanted more for her and even her private education couldn't keep her away.

The night she met Sean, he had been fighting and she had to meet her father at the King's Arms at the end of Pennyfields in East London. As soon as she saw him, his bulging muscles and his crystal blue eyes, she fell for him. He knew it would be a risk to have a relationship with a girl out of the tradition but he was sick of the way the girls teased the boys and decided to wait until he met the right girl.

Charlotte was exactly what he had been waiting for. She also had blonde hair and with the help of expensive highlights, it made her look almost Scandinavian. She had her father hard blue eyes, the image of Mason and always under his watchful eye, but it didn't stop Sean, he fell in love with her the moment they shook hands. He proposed a month later and the wedding was set for three months after that. Mason just hoped he would be home to be there.

ʊʊʊ

Holly had gone to bed, she cried herself to sleep and wished Ben could just hold her and tell her everything was going to be alright. But how could it be? She knew as well as Ethan that having a baby could cause problems for them both, after all, where was the father for one thing? She didn't even know if he had been returned to England or buried in a 'poor man's' grave on the Island of Jersey. Her heart felt as though it was breaking all over again, but she couldn't keep being the victim, she had to take control at some point.

The new house would certainly be big enough to raise a child, the last little bit of Ben she had left. She never even had a picture, when the child grew, it would have questions and how could she tell them the truth? Jock could still be looking for, he could search forever and one day he may find her and if he did, the child would be bate to him, an evil sadistic man.

Over the next few days she hardly left the house, one thing for sure was the constant nausea made her feel so useless, she could keep nothing down in the morning, nothing at all. Ethan began to worry, Mark said he would drive down, but how long would it take before he would arrive with all the answers like he'd had so many times already?

Ethan made her lemon tea late one afternoon, he had searched on line for some solutions to morning sickness and someone recommended it. He gently knocked on her door and slowly pushed it open. She was curled up on the huge bed with a sheet over her legs, holding herself across the middle, the only position she felt comfort in.

"Holly," he touched her shoulder, she jumped and opened her eyes, "sorry, I didn't mean to scare you, I made this for you."

"Thanks," she grumbled and sat up, the nausea had passed for now and her throat felt dry. "What time is it?"

"Uh, it's almost three. Mark called he is coming tomorrow so he might have some suggestions as to what we could do."

"I know what I should do and I know what I want to do, unfortunately they aren't the same," she grimaced. She sipped the tea, it was hot and refreshed her mouth.

"How long does morning sickness last?" he asked, the one thing he didn't look for on the internet.

"I wish it were just morning, it started off in the afternoon and now it's almost all day." She scoffed.

"Maybe you should see a doctor, something could be…wrong." He suggested, concerned,

"I know," she frowned.

He left her alone as she seemed to not want to talk much more. After a warm, relaxing, bubble filled  bath, she walked down stairs, Ethan was on the phone. His classes were due to start in a week also and as he laughed and talked with a perfect American accent, Holly wondered if they should go their own way.

Maybe buying the house was premature now and maybe she should have just continued driving and disappeared somewhere else, somewhere away from Mark and Ethan, her two big brother types that she really had no need for. Although she enjoyed Mark's company, he always seemed to be holding something back, she could tell. He never talked about himself, he seemed too private and that put her a little on edge whenever he was around.

After another day of thinking, she went to bed early. That night though, she couldn't sleep a wink. She lay awake in the darkness with the crickets drilling into her head from outside the window. It didn't help that she had already slept for four hours.

Ethan had gone out to a bar for pre-college drinks with a few of the students he met when he enrolled, so she was home alone. It made her wonder that at least if she had a baby, she would never be alone again. She decided that she needed to know how far gone she was before she could truly think about anything. As soon as she got up the next day, she made a call to the number given to her by the kind lady in the pharmacy.

Her appointment was booked for ten, she activated her medical insurance card, set up by Alex and showered and dressed. Her jeans already felt tight as she zipped them up. A bulge had already begun to form; maybe she was too late for the other option anyway. Secretly, she hoped she was. That way she would not have to fight Mark and Ethan on the issue.

After a quick examination and an ultra sound, it was confirmed, fourteen weeks pregnant,

"But I can't be fourteen weeks, I mean, I had periods, I think I have only missed one." Holly frowned as she dressed.

"Sometimes the body is cheated into thinking that you're not pregnant and some women can have periods right through the term," Dr Shelly Munroe explained. She pushed her glasses back up her nose. Her dark hair was tied up in a ponytail and her friendly, brown eyes sparkled. "Listen, uh, Miss Long, I can understand how you are feeling, I see that you have put single on your form."

"I am. The uh, father was killed in an accident, I wasn't married to him so I am not a widow. There wasn't another option I could choose. I thought it was stress."

"Are you okay? I mean, I have an excellent counsellor for bereavement issues."

"No, no, I am fine, all part of his," she pointed up, "plan, I suppose, so what about vitamins?" she asked in a perfect English accent.

"You're not a native American, are you?" Dr Munroe asked, Holly glared into her eyes.

"I uh, I immigrated to New England a few years back, with my parents and my brother."

"So, are you from Old England?" she pressed.

"Yes," Holly swallowed, *busted*, she thought.

"I knew that wasn't a full on Mass accent," she smiled, "Did you not want to move back home then?"

"Are you kidding? Three hundred days of rain a year, smog, so thick you can't see the other side of the street, there is nothing back there for me, not anymore."

"Sorry, I didn't mean to pry; you just seem…like you are a little lost."

"I have been raising my brother since my parents died, then my uh, boyfriend, but I am getting there."

"Are you ready to be a mother?" she asked, Holly snapped her head up.

"I don't really have a choice now, do I?"

"You can terminate up to sixteen weeks, if you wanted."

"Dr Munroe, I have lost everything, I cannot just terminate this baby, I just can't."

"Well, okay. I'll write down a list of some prenatal vitamins you will need to take and some pre natal classes if you feel like it," she then smiled. "I am here if you need me, Holly, okay? I know I am just a doctor, but I am a good listener, so if you need a girly chat some time, just call," she then handed her a black and white picture. "One for the album," she said. Holly looked at the tiny fingers beginning to form and a tear escaped.

"Thank you…for everything," Holly smiled and brushed away the tear.


She gazed at the picture as she sat in her car outside the doctor's office. Dr Munroe seemed genuine enough, she just hoped that she didn't delve too much into Holly's fragile history made up by Alex, Mark's lawyer friend. As she drove out of the parking lot her eyes fell on the furniture store across the street, it had a butter scotch yellow leather couch, it was huge and looked comfortable, she had to go and have a look at it.

"Can I help you, ma'am?" a young looking sales assistant smiled. He was tall with rust coloured hair and green eyes.

"Uh, yes, I want this couch." She stated.

"Okay, I'll get the order form."

"No, you don't understand, I want this couch," Holly smiled.

"Well, it's our display model, ma'am, hundreds of butts have sat on it."

"Yes, but I take it those butts were actually dressed when they sat on the couch."

"Yes," he blushed, he couldn't have been more than a teenager. "Let me talk to my manager."

"Okay," she nodded and rubbed her hand across the back of it.

An older man approached with a smile, "Hey, so, my colleague Sam tells me you set your mind on this one," he said.

"That's right," she affirmed. "I have just bought a new house and this will go perfect in the living room."

"It usually takes twelve weeks to order," he explained, she rolled her eyes. "Okay, so if you take my only display model, how will I sell anymore?"

"How much is it?"

"Three thousand dollars," he answered.

"I'll give you five, will that compensate you enough?" she asked.

"You want to pay me five grand for a three grand couch?" he frowned.

"Yes, I really want this and I would like it delivered this weekend," he looked back at Sam, "do we have a deal?"

"Uh, okay, we have a deal," he smiled. "Sam, get on to Milano, order us another display model."

"Thank you," Holly smiled. "So, what else do you have?"


Ten thousand dollars later she left and drove home, Ethan was sunbathing in the back garden and she poured out two iced cold drinks and took them out to him. She handed him a glass of soda and sat beside him on the sun lounger.

"What's the verdict?" he asked.

"It's too late for an abortion," she lied, well, it was for her, she'd seen it now and it had fingers already.

"So, you are going to have it?" he sat up.

"I have no choice now, Ethan. I understand if you want to go or would rather keep your distance, we'll be fine."

"I told you that I would support you, Holly; don't think you are on your own." He sipped his drink.

"Thanks," she smiled slightly.

"Mark is on his way, so…"

"Great and I expect he wants me to get rid of it as well." She spat.

"He just said it may complicate things, he'll be alright. Besides, it's not like he's the father, is it?"

"No," she grimaced as her mind drifted to the last words she shared with Ben.

After a sandwich for lunch she went up to her room, she needed to clean it. After all, it was Mark's house and with laundry all over the floor, he might not appreciate having them there if they didn't respect the house. So, she scrubbed the bathrooms and changed all of the beds too. The second floor laundry came in handy that afternoon and she made the most of it.

When she finally came down the stairs, Mark had already arrived and he and Ethan were drinking beer out on the back deck by the pool. He smiled as she came out, but it wasn't the smile she was used too, it seemed full of disappointment. There was nothing she would or could do about it. She sat at the table with them,

"How are you, Holly?" he asked politely.

"Fine, thank you," she replied. "And how are you?"

"Oh, I'm alright, always am," he smiled slightly again. Her integrity always struck him and almost knocked him over; she seemed the most genuine person he knew. "So, we have a little situation now then?"

"It's not something that was planned, Mark," she said tartly.

"I know, are you sure you want this Lis... I mean, Holly?"

"Of course I am," she stiffened and sat up slightly. "Look, I realise that this is a complication, Mark, but I will be fine."

"And if they find you here with the baby, what then?"

"Maybe I'll just give them the rest back and they'll let us live," she smiled.

"But I am busting my ass looking or a new buyer for you," he snapped.

"I know, I do appreciate everything, Mark but..."

"I don't think you do," he frowned. She swallowed, "You don't see how dangerous it is for you now, you can't trust anyone."

"Including you?" she asked, he thought for a few moments and then he smirked,

"Especially me," he winked his eye and she smiled. "It's nothing to do with me what you choose to do, Holly, I am just trying to look out for you, just as I promised Ben I would," that cut deeper than she'd liked. "Sorry to bring him up."

"I know," she lowered her eyes. "Can I show you something?" she asked and went inside to find her bag. Mark and Ethan followed her to the kitchen, "Here," she handed Mark the picture of the baby. He looked at it and then at her,

"That is awesome, Holly," he grinned feeling a little mushy inside.

"Do you see how I would be getting rid of a baby, not a peanut size egg, a baby with eyes and fingers, Mark? I can't do that."

"No, I suppose you can't," he admitted.

# Ten

ᚥᚥᚥ

Friday night Vic and Mason had to meet a kid called Fynn, he had been bragging that his sister had friends coming over from Dublin and one was a pretty girl fitting Lisa's description. It made Mason tingle to think they might actually have a lead, another week has flown by in that motel, he was about to skin Julian alive and pull Vic's balls out of his throat.

The constant fighting and sarcastic comments were getting to be too much for him to stand a moment longer than he had to do. Since his rant at Jock, Vic's filthy mouth had re-emerged and Julian was on the sour end of his dirty tongue daily. They went back to Flannigan's and waited for Stacey the blonde and attractive bar maid from Rosslaire to point Fynn out to them.

They sat at the bar and Vic peeled at the label of his beer while they waited. He had a huge fight with Sheila before they left, she was leaving for their Spanish holiday the following morning and wanted him there so they could go together, he wished he was there too. As much as his wife irritated him, he loved her and was actually looking forward to a week in the sun, lounging by the pool. Instead he was stuck in Boston with a whiney brat and a grumpy old geezer. Not his idea of a holiday at all, especially when they cashed in their insurance to pay for it.

"Cat got ya tongue, mate?" Mason nudged him.

"What are we gonna do when we find this kid?"

"I don't know, I want to see him first," Mason swigged at his beer. "He's late."

"Typical," Vic sighed and drank some of his beer. Stacey placed two more in front of them and nodded towards the door. Mason paid her the fifty dollars he promised and they watched as Fynn approached the bar. He ordered his usual, as he put it in his tinny Irish accent and smiled at them.

"Do I know you?" he asked.

"No, son," Mason smiled. "I'll get that for you," he paid for his drink.

"Cheers," Fynn nodded wearily, "so, you are English then?"

"That's right, is that a Dublin accent?"

"Sure is," Fynn smiled proudly. "What brings you to Boston?"

"Well, my mate here is looking for his niece; she ran away from home, I'm just helping him out."

"Oh yeah, she came here then, did she?"

"So we were told, the thing is her mum is ill and well, my mate don't hold much hope out for his sister, so we have to find her and bring her home before she pops her clogs."

"I hope you find her."

"So do we, son, so do we," Mason drank some of his beer, "Don't suppose you know of any girls from the UK or Ireland even, arriving in the last few weeks, she might be looking for work or help, she may have been with a man."

"No, sorry," he glared at them both, Vic let out a huge playing along sigh. "My sister had a friend come over; I could try and find out for you."

"My mate is prepared to pay for any information that can help us find her."

"Alright, look, give me an hour and I will see what I can do," he lifted his drink and drank the rest, "thanks for the drink."

"You are welcome," Mason winked at him. "Thanks, son," he looked at Vic again and then left the bar.

"So, that's your big plan, we lie and hope he comes back with something?"

"Well, I was all up for pulling finger nails out, but I thought I might try the friendly approach for a change." He grinned.

"And if it doesn't work?"

"Then we can get your pliers out," he smiled. "Cheer up, me old China, we could be going home soon."

"Yeah, she's going to divorce me for this, I hope you are happy," he moaned.

"She is getting a bit old for you me old mucker, she'd be doin' you a favour, you might find a nice little bit of crumpet," he nudged him. "A nice bit of stuff to put a smile on ya face and iron your Y-fronts."

"Sod off," Vic smiled.

Time ticked on and the hour was up, as they were about to leave, Fynn came back, his black hair was stuck to his face with water, and they didn't know it had rained outside. He smiled as he approached and ushered them to a seat at the back,

"So, when you said you'd pay…"

"I will pay, do you have something for me?" Vic asked keenly.

"I might," Fynn smiled, "it depends on how much you are prepared to pay."

"Well, how about we start with a tonne?" Mason asked.

"A tonne?" Fynn frowned.

"Yeah, hundred quid," Mason elaborated.

"Hmm," Fynn frowned rubbing his nicotine stained fingers over his forehead.

"Alright, we'll go to three hundred and that would give you nearly six hundred dollars, mate?" Vic added.

"Done," Fynn held out his hand to shake it.

"We'll hear what you have first." Mason leaned closer towards him.

"Fine, my sister helped a couple of friends a few weeks back, a guy about twenty five and a girl a bit younger. She got them a car and then they left, she said she thought they were heading for Vegas, here," he slid a piece of paper over to them. Vic glanced around and lifted the paper, "It's the license plate number of the car she got them. You might be able to use it."

"Cheers, mate," Vic smiled and handed him a bundle of twenty pound notes, "my sister will be happy."

"Family is important, mate, and this is no place for a young girl alone," he picked up the money and stood. "Nice doing business with you, boys," he smiled.

"Likewise, son," Mason replied.


Back at the motel with a bottle of the finest whisky the liquor store had, Mason and Vic poured out three glasses, Julian smiled too, this room had become his prison cell, so the prospect that they were leaving cheered him up no end.

"Drink up, kid, it'll put hairs on ya chest," Mason grinned.

"I have more hair on my chest than you have on your entire body, old man," Julian replied smartly.

Vic snickered, "I wouldn't bet on it, Mason is known as the bear in his house."

"What about you, Vic?" Julian smiled, "Are you the bald, silver back gorilla?"

"How did you know?" Mason grinned, "But then his misses does look like she's from Planet of the Apes."

"That's 'cos his misses is Medusa and he's jealous," Vic smiled.

"I am surprised you and Sheila are still going strong," Julian grinned.

"Oh, we are, mate, bloody strong, just going in opposite directions," Vic sighed and sat on the chair, "Come on then, fire this thing up and trace this registration number, I need my beauty sleep."

"We won't argue with that," Mason laughed.


The following morning they were sat in a small diner up the street from their motel. The plate had come up a blank and they were all hung-over. The waitress placed three cups of black coffee in front of them.

"I'd give my eye teeth for a decent cup of Rosie," Mason frowned.

"I second that," Vic groaned, "and it's in a bloody black cup, I hate drinking out of black cups."

"What difference does it make what colour cup you drink out of?" Julian asked.

"I don't know, it just tastes like shit out of a black cup. The trouble and strife changed the kitchen a few months back and everything is black and white, I made her buy me a white cup, 'cos I ain't using the black ones." He lifted his coffee and sniffed it, "I can't even face that," he slammed the cup down splashing hot coffee over the table.

"Watch it, mate," Mason snapped and threw some napkins down on the mess allowing them to soak it up. "Black cups do not affect the bloody flavour of a cuppa, Vic; you really have got some issues." He added.

"Yeah, I am staring at them both, right now," Vic snapped.

"Right then, I suppose I better go and tell your uncle the good news," Mason groaned.

"Let's speak to Fynn again," Julian suggested, "maybe you two can push some of that weight around that you have been bragging about since we got here."

"I'll push you around, laughing boy," Mason snarled as he stood. "He gave us all he could."

"Yeah, well, I ain't byin' it," Julian frowned. "I think he knows more he just needs some of your gentle persuasion."

"How about I gentle persuasion you right round your left ear hole? You cheeky little Git," he warned, Vic rolled his eyes, he felt too sick to push anything around. Mason left the table.

"All I am saying, Victor is…"Julian began as soon as Mason was out of ear shot.

"Julian, shut the fuck up, alright? My head is bangin' and I have not got the patience for you or your cocky little theories, like I said, experience speaks volumes."

"Well, we are not supposed to be writing a best seller, are we? We are meant to be finding that bitch with my uncle's stones."

"Halle-bloody-luiah, he finally gets it," Vic smiled.

"Right then, we're goin' home," Mason announced as he approached them, "Come on, Vic, you can have a hot cup of Rosie on the plane, mate."

"You mean that Scots twat said come home, nothing else?" Vic frowned.

"He's got a bit of aggro back home and needs to lay low, who am I to argue?" Mason smiled with an over the top shrug.

"I really wish you'd stop calling my uncle names," Julian moaned as he stood.

"Listen to me you jumped up little prick," Mason snapped, "I have had just about enough of you this week, alright? I feel like shit and you are not helping, so unless you have something constructive to say, I would keep that trap of yours shut, before I snap your jaw in half and shut you up permanently."

"What about my uncle?" Julian smirked.

"Like I said before, we could always say the sharks got ya, plus you can't speak if your mouth is wired shut and I break all of your fingers," Vic winked his eye and followed Mason out. Julian left the money for the coffees and ran to catch them up.

They sat in the departure lounge a day later as that was the earliest flight they could get. The flight was at four and they have about another thirty minutes to wait before boarding. Vic had bought Sheila and expensive bottle of perfume by way of an apology even though he knew he'd be sleeping on the sofa for God knows how long and will have no say whatsoever on what she spends the money on for a few weeks. She would be home from their Spanish holiday in a few days and he knew it wouldn't be pretty.

Mason saw panic on his mates face and knew it was best not to upset him anymore. He felt bad for dragging him States when his marriage could be in jeopardy, he knew how hard Sheila was with Vic and that she was the real reason he gave up being a heavy in the first place. So, if she found out the truth, not only would she make Vic's life not worth living, she do her best to upset Monica and then Mason would be on a park bench too.

He had bigger things to worry about though, Charlie's wedding was a week away and he knew that Pikey idiot would be whisking her off the Emerald Isle to live and there wasn't anything he could do about it.

Two double whiskeys and a glass of red wine after their dinner and Vic and Mason slept for most of the flight home. Julian tapped away at his lap top but he was anxious. He had waited a few years to finally work for his uncle, the first job he gets and he screws it up. He genuinely wanted to make something of his life and with the lack of jobs for college drop outs, he had nothing else to look forward to.

Back to his dingy, roach infested flat in Camden where Matilda and Ginny were his prostitute neighbours and he would have to spend endless nights listening to them banging away at their clients through hardboard walls.

At least the flight home was a British airline company and that meant he could have a drink to help lighten his mood. Although with Vic and Mason as his new enemies, he was looking forward to seeing the back of them.

Vic drove them back towards the city and they went straight to Jock's office at the junk yard just down the road from the local cricket ground. Jock groaned a hello as they came in and stood in front of him. On the desk sat an envelope of crumpled bank notes, he pushed it towards Mason.

"I always pay my way," Jock said amicably.

"Well, we didn't deliver, so…" Mason frowned.

"No, but I know you have your daughter's wedding coming up, you worked hard for it. Can't let those Gypsies show us up now, can we?"

"Suppose not," Mason frowned at Vic who had realised what this meant. They were now in Jock's debt which meant they would have to deliver Prince Charlie's balls on a silver plate if he asked them to.

"So, you go on now, we'll talk soon," Jock half smiled at them before they left hit office.

Vic held his tongue for all of three seconds, as soon as the door shut he started.

"You know what this means now, don't ya?" he asked opening the car door. Mason frowned at him, "We're his, he can snap his fingers and we'll have to jump."

"We did a job and he paid us," Mason groaned.

"Blokes like Jock do not pay for nothing, he's got something up his sleeve and I know we will pay back big time." Vic sighed as he climbed in the car.

"At the moment, mate," Mason replied. "I couldn't give a monkey's what his motives are. I have bigger things than that Scots twat on my plate."

Jock watched them drive off and turned to Julian, "I want you to look something up for me, laddie, can you do that?" Julian nodded and Jock handed him a piece of paper. "Let me know what you find out," he winked his eye and placed a pile of cash in his hand. "Find somewhere else to live too, that flat is a bigger tip than this place."

ϖϖϖ

Mark stayed the weekend with Holly and Ethan, by the time he left, he agreed with her, having an abortion would be out of the question. He knew she would never live with the guilt after and he couldn't bear to face her knowing what he had made her do, if he had been able to convince her it was right and safer. A baby would thwart matters, but at the end of the day, it was her life.

Holly felt a little sadness after he left, having Mark around always seemed to make her feel safe. Plus she knew the next time she would see him, she would have moved into her own house. Ethan had a date that evening and for the first time since Ben died, Holly wondered if she'd ever be capable of falling in love again.

Over the next few days the sale was finalised and she was given the go ahead to get the furniture delivered and make the house a home so that she could move in.

Dr Munroe had sent her a list of prenatal clinic appointments and a baby name book, she called the office.

"Can I speak with Dr Munroe please?" she asked.

"Please hold," the voice said.

"Dr Munroe."

"Hi, it's Holly Long, I just wanted to thank you for the book."

"Oh, it's something I had lying around the office," she explained. "How are you?"

"Uh, sick of feeling sick," she confessed with a smile.

"Try some ginger tea, it might settle it down a bit," she suggested.

"I will, thank you."

"You are welcome, take care now." She said.

"I promise," she smiled. "Oh, before you go, I am moving this weekend, would you like my new address?"

"Sure," she replied and wrote down Holly's new address. Holly sighed after she hung up the phone, she knew one thing, she needed to make some friends or her life was going to get increasingly lonely.

# Eleven

"Now are you sure about this?" Jock asked, Julian nodded his head. "Good lad," he grinned. Then he looked at the other two men in his office, "Right, looks like you are going to pay our Mr Hobbs a visit in Houston."

"Houston?" One of them frowned, he had skin head and looked almost bald with a gold tooth.

"Yes, you know where Houston is, right? Cowboys, oil tycoons?" He nodded his head and lowered it slightly feeling humiliated, this was his first job though, he needed to keep his mouth shut and try not to look like he was such a prat. "Mr Hobbs has been looking for someone to buy some gems, should have been a little more careful," he snarled sitting back in his chair and resting his elbows on the arms. "Stupid cowboy," he scoffed.

"So, we're going to Texas?" the other asked.

"Keep up, Sonny Jim," Jock snapped. "Your flights are booked for Wednesday, she has days left, the sneaky little bitch," Julian glared at his uncle not liking what he was seeing. "Good work, Julian, I am proud of you, son," he handed him another wad of notes.

"She looks a diamond, mate," Vic smiled as Charlie danced her first dance with her new husband. Mason grinned proudly. She did look beautiful in her diamante encrusted, white wedding dress, her curly, blonde hair, bouncing off her shoulders. Monica cried with Sheila, they had cried all day too much to drink and now they were so drunk, all they could do was cry. The dance was over and the DJ announced the father daughter dance. Mason handed his pint to Vic and took Charlie's hand.

"Are you alright, sweetheart?" he asked her as they danced.

"Yes, thank you, Dad, it's the best," she replied.

"You look the bee's knees," he smiled proudly.

"I feel it," she agreed. "I am going to miss you and Mum."

"We'll miss you too, but you have your own life to live, love, he better look after you."

"He will, Vic has already given him a talking to," she said rolling her eyes. "I am just so happy, Dad."

"And that makes me happy," he smiled, "just remember where we are, love eh, keep in touch and if he ever lays a finger on you, Sheila and Vic got you some stainless steel pans with a ten year guarantee, you could always clobber him over the head with one."

"What are you like, Dad?" she giggled.

Considering there were over a hundred Gypsies at the reception, there was no trouble. Only those with an invitation could get in and others dared to try with Bruce and Phil on the door, they knew better. Both were as big as sheds and looked like pit bull dogs, almost foaming at the mouth. Although they were on their best behaviour and would only use it if provoked, when a scrawny bloke came up to them wanting to see Vic and Mason, they sent for the two men.

"What is it?" Mason asked approaching the three men.

"This bloke wants a word," Phil snarled.

"Julian, what do you want?" Vic asked.

"We need to talk, it's about the girl," Julian explained.

"Inside, this better be good, it's my daughter's wedding day," Mason moaned marching him through the lobby into a room. He closed the door behind them and Vic folded his arms across his chest. "Right then, what's going on?"

"He had me look up few things after you left the other day," he explained. "I hacked into an e-mail account belonging to a Mark Hobbs, he's a guy my uncle uses to shift stuff State side. Well, it seems he is looking for a buyer to take some gems off his hands."

"I knew it, I knew that cocky shit had something up his sleeve," Vic moaned.

"So, what's he doing about it?" Mason then asked.

"He's sending a pair of rookies over to take care of it, the Evans brothers," he shrugged.

"Meaning," Mason shrugged.

"Meaning that girl you are worried about, well, I'd say her days are numbered. They are going to meet a couple of nasty arse bastards in Houston and she is in trouble."

"For fuck sake," Vic snapped under his breath. "We gotta find her first, Mason, they'll kill her."

"We'd better bloody pack again, what do we tell the misses?" Mason asked.

"Buggered if I know, mate, she still ain't forgiven me for that last jaunt. Fishing trip?" he offered.

"Vic, your language is diabolical, me old son," Mason shook his head.

"It's Jock, whenever he's around I can't help myself, it's like, he presses this button in my head and I want to hurt someone or swear. The last I heard, you can't get thrown in nick for swearing."

"Don't you kid yourself," Julian sighed. "So, what are we going to do?"

"You are going home, son," Mason frowned. "If Jock finds out you grassed him up to us, he'll have your knee caps, so unless you want to spend your life blowjob height, I suggest you go home and don't tell anyone you were here. I'll keep you informed," he promised and walked him to the door, "Now remember, Julian, you need to keep that trap shut and let us do the work," Mason then held out his hand. "You're a top bloke, mate, that girl does not deserve all this shit."

"Alright, Mason," Julian nodded shaking his hand and feeling quite important to these men he had actually started to look up to and respect. They were the best in the business and been around enough to still use their savvy more often than not.

Mason turned to Vic and they walked back into the wedding in time to see Charlie throw her bouquet and about thirty girls rip it to shreds fighting over it.

"I don't fuckin' believe it," Mason sighed, "hundred and ninety quid that thing cost me."

"And you said my language is bad."

There is no way you should have to wake up to an argument the Sunday morning after partying at a wedding until two in the morning, but Sheila could not believe her husband's sudden interest in golf, especially as he had always said it was the best way to ruin a good walk.

"I just don't buy it, Vic, you don't even like sport, any sport, accept bloody boxing and you must think I'm a monkey's aunt if you think I will believe the crap that's spilling out of your mouth."

"Sheila," he groaned and turned over to face the wall, "Can we talk about this later?"

"No, you are flying out tonight and I want to know the bloody truth," with his head pounding he opened his eyes slowly and turned to face his wife. "Well?" she asked sharply folding her arms. She still had her curlers in and smudged eyeliner under her eyes.

"Well, what?" he snapped.

"Where are you going?"

"Florida, Mason's mate Tony has a villa on a golf course and we can go for free. I can't let him down, love, you know that."

"Yeah, I forget there's three in this marriage," she snapped and pushed off the bed covers, Vic buried his face in the pillow as she pulled open the curtains revealing a blinding sun. "If you go, I won't be here when you get back," she wrapped her dressing gown around her body and stormed from the bedroom. He looked at the alarm clock,

"Seven o'clock," he yelled, "you woke me up at seven o'bloody clock on a Sunday," he then threw the clock against the wall smashing it over the bedroom floor.

"Did she believe you?" Mason asked as they entered terminal three at Heathrow airport. Vic just glared at him, "Monica neither, bloody women, remind me, why did we get married again?"

Vic shrugged, "I don't know and when you find out let me know, I will never be able to figure women out. Sometimes I wish I was women to better understand what makes her tick, honestly, mate, she baffles me." He sighed as they joined the line of travellers to check in.

"You wish you were a woman? And you warned me not to bend over in that queers pub in Boston," Mason chuckled. "I don't want to understand Monica, in fact, I would be happy if I never did. First it was PMS and now it's the menopause, we don't have to go through that crap and that's the way I like it."

"But if they didn't have all of that, what would they moan about then?" Vic asked.

"Us," they said together.

"Still, at least I get to sort of use my retirement present," Mason added as they reached the check in counter, placing his unused golf bag and clubs on the floor.

"Yeah, but not for golf, eh?" Vic grinned.

"Are you checking these clubs, sir?" the girl asked.

"I don't need to check them, love, I already know they're clean," Mason smiled confidently.

"She meant did you want to check them as luggage, mate?" Vic winked at the girl whose face had turned crimson.

"Well, in that case," Mason frowned, "yes please."

Julian had provided them with as much information he had with regard to Mark Hobbs. It was vague, but surely someone in Houston would have heard of this Mark Hobbs. Vic seemed to like the idea of going to Texas, he had always fancied himself as a cowboy and planned to buy a huge ten gallon hat as soon as they could find a shop.

As an avid fan of the TV series Dallas in the eighties, to actually feel the heat of the Wild West had some appeal for him. He didn't mind the southerners, as he called them. Mason just hoped Monica would forgive him for leaving two days after Charlie left home. Before she moved out he could go away and knew she had company, but now she would be alone in the house.

Julian promised to keep an eye on things and Vic had to admit the kid had turned a corner on Respect Street. When you are ready to grass your own arsehole uncle up, you are worthy of a little respect. Providing you didn't act like a twat and lose it all again.

This ten hour flight would be a long one, so they both filled up on double whiskeys and closed their eyes.

ᚹᚹᚹ

# Twelve

College for Ethan was better than he expected, he was a popular student. Word of their fortune spread fast around campus and he had already lied saying they had a lottery win, something that had pissed Holly off no end.

They had moved into the new house and Holly was rapidly filling it with furniture to make it a home. Mark had stayed in touch and had found another buyer prepared to take some more of the stones off her hands, which pleased her, because she felt sure the fact that they were sat in the bank added to her stress.

He had driven down again to see the new house and as Holly had paid cleaners to leave Mark's house as they found it, he would get his keys back too.

Ethan finished at three and picked up fresh bread on his way back to the new house. He found Holly asleep on the sofa, as she always did in the afternoons; the pregnancy left her exhausted although she felt that it was boredom. Even the excitement of seeing Mark again couldn't prevent her from needing a nap. Ethan let her sleep and started peeling potatoes for the huge meal Holly had planned by way of a thank you to Mark for the lone of his house.

Her pre-natal appointment had provided her with another picture and she got to hear the train track heartbeat. Her bump was tiny, but still a bump and it was plainly obvious that she was pregnant. Since the doctor confirmed, she seemed to have sprouted outwards. She even had to shop for maternity clothes and allowed herself to buy a few items for the baby.     While she was at the mall she bumped into her doctor and one of the nurses, they had lunch together and loved it, the female company was definitely something she needed and it further confirmed how lonely she was. She desperately needed female friends and accepted the offer of prenatal classes to help her meet other expectant mums.

Ethan singing to U2 *'With Or Without You'* woke her. His accent was stronger than ever and she could hear his Irish twang as he belted out the words reminding her that he was still Rory, just as she was still Lisa.

She followed the noise to the kitchen where he was washing the huge chicken she had bought. He danced around with the chicken and as he spun around he saw her smiling at him,

"Afternoon, sunshine," he grinned and turned down the music, "I love that song." He added dropping the chicken into the oven tray.

"Yeah, U2 are great," she agreed.

"Do you need something to drink; I could make you a cup of tea, kettle has only just boiled?"

"Sure, thanks," she yawned.

"Are you still tired?" he asked her pouring water onto a teabag in a cup.

"No, well, yes, I am always tired," she sighed and sat at the table, "Do you think Mark will like the house?" she asked.

"Sure he will," he smiled and placed a hot cup of milky tea in front of her. "We're gonna need to find that store again, we're almost out."

"Sorry, it's the only thing that settles my stomach."

"I know," he winked at her. "Lis…I mean, Holly, this is going to work, right? I mean, now with the baby coming and all?"

"I hope so." She replied and sipped her tea, "Look, my doctor bought the story, why shouldn't anyone else?"

"Yeah, s'pose you're right, what time is the guest of honour arriving?"

"Uh, after five is all he said."

"I am meant to be taking this girl out tonight," he frowned.

"Oh, well, you can if you want, I am sure Mark and I will find something to talk about."

"He likes you, ya know," he smiled, she felt her face redden, "I know you think it's too soon, but you could do a lot worse."

"A lot worse than a stolen jewel dealer, who won't even tell me his real name," she stood. "I knew Ben was an asshole from the first time we met, I knew what I was getting into and I could have walked away anytime I wanted, but I didn't and now he's dead, dead, Rory, so if I was looking for someone else, it would not be Mark Hobbs, however charming he may be, he is still crooked."

"Crooked, but he would look after you and the baby, you'd want for nothing."

"And it's because of the baby we could never be more than friends," she sighed and left the room.

She ran up to her room and shut the door, her huge four poster bed sat in the middle and looked almost as if it had come right out of a romantic novel, the swags of chiffon swooped down from the corners and the new carpet felt soft under her feet.

She showered and dressed in a new light blue dress bought that day. She wore white shoes and pinned the sides of her hair up. Every time she caught a glimpse of herself she felt awful, Mark liked her and worse than that, she liked him too. But it had been only weeks since she left Ben's lifeless body in that room back in Jersey. How could she even conceive of the idea of Mark Hobbs in her life as more than just a friend?

Ethan knocked gently on her door; she snapped back into reality and continued brushing her hair in the mirror,

"Holly, Mark's downstairs," he called through the door.

"Okay, thanks," she replied, took a deep breath and stood. When she came out of her room, he stood back and smiled approvingly. "Stop it," she demanded leaving him leaning against the wall.

"Hey," Mark grinned as she came down the stairs, "Look at this place, it's fantastic."

"I am glad you like it," she smiled.

"You look great," he mused with a lopsided smile.

"I look fat," she amended, "but thanks anyway." She led him through the house. "Let me give you the grand tour."

She showed him the many rooms and the garden out the back. Her pool and hot tub that she didn't even know was there until after she had bought it.

"You are the talk of town," he said as they sat on the deck. He sipped a cold beer and she drank her tea.

"I am, why?" she frowned.

"Well, this place for one thing," he replied, "you need to stop flashing your wealth around so flamboyantly." He cautioned.

"Wow, that's a huge word, so, I have to sit on that amount of money for the rest of my life?"

"While that idiot is still looking for you anyway," he relied. She took a deep breath, "Sorry, I am just worried that you will draw too much attention to you and Ethan. I promised Ben I would look after you and I am doing a crap job." She gazed into his eyes briefly and rubbed her hand over her bump, "How is the baby?"

"Fine, I suppose, I am just bloody knackered all of the time and rapidly running out of tea bags. All I am craving is my mum's Yorkshire puddings, she made the best you know, light and fluffy."

"I tried one once, when I came over to see Ben years ago. We went to a pub in London and had roast beef, I couldn't believe you had baked pancake batter with a roast dinner," he chuckled. "And what is it with lard sandwiches? Gross."

"Lard sandwiches," she frowned. "Oh, you mean beef dripping, hated the stuff, but my Nan loves it on crusty bread with salt and pepper." She smiled as she remembered watching her Nan sat at the table and sprinkling her dripping with salt and pepper and then folding the bread over before taking a bight.

"You miss your family, don't you," he stated.

She nodded her head, "You have no idea how hard it is to be here and not pick up the phone to talk to them and let them know I am alright."

"I know, I had to leave my roots too, remember, but you just have to do it, especially now. Look, Jock will give up, trust me. He'll get bored of looking for you and maybe then you might be able to contact your home, but until then…"

"Until then," she sighed. "Anyway, we could sit here all night and talk, but I have a dinner to cook and serve. Would you like another beer?"

"I shouldn't, I need to drive back to my house."

"You could have one of the rooms here, if you wanted to."

"You are so typically English, polite and generous," he smiled, "thank you, in that case, yes, I would love another beer."

ʊʊʊ

The seat belt light finally went off with a ping and they could stand up, Mason tied up his shoes and Vic removed the hand luggage for them both, this time they were travelling under the names Arthur Daily and Terry McCann, the other passports they owned. They felt sure that alarm bells would ring if they used the same names as before. The golf clubs proved to be a handy prop where immigration was concerned. The officer who cleared them even gave them a few golf courses to visit while in Houston. As they stepped out into the bright sunshine with a perfect blue sky above Vic smiled inhaling some warm air,

"This is the life," he grinned following the kid from the car rental counter across a packed car lot.

"Makes Poplar look like the slums in Calcutta," Mason agreed.

"I wish Sheila would come over here, she'd love it," Vic said

"What about all that 'I hate the Yanks' crap?" Mason frowned.

"Well, we're down south now, I like the south it's in me bones," Vic explained.

"How many whiskeys did you have?"

"I don't know, but I think we cleared 'em out," Vic shrugged.

"The only thing you got in your bones, mate, is car fumes, asbestos, and pollution."

"Well, let's hope they don't do a blood test on me then, they might want me to go to NASA or summink."

"You wish, mate," Mason grinned as the young man turned and handed him the car keys.

"There you go, sir; she's got a full tank of gas…"

"That's great, son, but we can't drive on fart power," Vic chuckled.

"Take no notice of him, mate, he's had one too many," Mason winked and handed him a five dollar bill. "Now then, how do we get out of here again?"

"Where are you headed?" he asked as he handed him the keys.

"Uh, well, we need to get to some office block near the docks," Vic explained and showed the guy the address.

"Just head in to the city and Main Avenue has a theatre on the corner. Turn down that street and I think that office is on the left."

"Thanks, son," Vic handed him another ten dollars.

"Thank you, sir, enjoy your stay."

"We will," Mason smiled.

They loaded up the small Chevrolet Neon and hit the road. Neither of them wanted to stop until they found Lisa, she was in danger and for the sake of a few gems she was not going to die.

Mason drove as Vic was still under the influence of the alcohol he had consume during the flight. When they hit the city, they followed the directions they were given and parked the car in the car lot of the Hobbs Corporation. They gazed up, the building went up into the pure blue sky.

"Flamin' heck," Vic gasped.

"This is Texas, Vic, everything is big here."

"That's not big, mate, that's enormous," Vic smiled.

Vic marvelled at the marble floor in the lobby of the building, an attractive blonde with stunning white teeth smiled,

"How can I help you today, sirs?" she asked politely.

"We would like to see Mr 'Obbs," Vic smiled.

"Uh, we don't have a Mr Obbs here I am afraid."

"It says his name over there, Miss, Mr Mark 'Obbs."

"Oh, you mean Mr Hobbs," she smiled emphasizing the *'H'*. "He is actually out of the office until Monday," she explained.

"Well, where is he then?" Mason frowned.

"I can't tell you that, Mr Hobbs is extremely private, sir, no one knows where he goes at the weekends."

"No one, so how do you get hold of him?"

"We page him," she replied.

"Can you page him, it is very important that we speak to him today?" Mason asked.

"I can ask his assistant to come and see you, would that help?"

"If that's your best offer," Mason sighed and they sat on the seats behind them. "How the hell can you run a bloody company and go AWOL whenever you want to?"

"Look at this place, I'd be shit scared to leave this and bugger off for the weekend, wouldn't you?" Vic asked gazing around.

"Yeah," Mason agreed.

"Hello, my name is Jay Lee," a tall man with dark brown hair smiled. He had blue eyes and a small rat shaped face. Vic didn't like him or the way he spoke through his nose, like he had a cold or something.

"What does the 'J' stand for?" Vic asked.

"Jay is my name, sir."

"Jay Lee," Vic grinned, "so, are you related to Bruce?"

"I don't believe I am," clearly missing the point. Vic rolled his eyes. "Can I ask what you would like to talk to Mr Hobbs about?"

"You can," Mason replied, "but it doesn't mean we are going to tell you."

"If that's how you want it," Jay frowned and turned to walk away.

"What my friend means is that we need to vet you first."

"Vet me?" Jay turned back to them, looked over at the receptionist and smiled. "I am not sure I know what you mean."

"Well, this is a very serious matter, sunshine, and we want to find out if you are a good egg or a bad egg," Mason explained.

"Maybe you should come to my office."

"Maybe we should," Mason stood, Vic joined them and they followed Jay to the glass elevator. He took them up to the thirtieth floor and led them to his office. Vic looked out of the window before he sat on a huge brown leather chair.

"Can I offer you two a beverage? I can have my secretary bring you some coffee or maybe some tea."

"Tea would be pucker, mate," Vic smiled.

"He means tea would be nice, thank you," Mason rephrased. Jay lifted his phone and ordered the tea.

"So, how can we be of service to you?" Jay asked.

"It is vital we speak with Mr Hobbs," Mason said and sat forward slightly,       "there seems to be a problem."

"A problem with what?" he frowned looking at each of them.

"With... look, mate, are you kosher?" Vic asked impatiently.

"I don't know what you mean I am afraid," Jay shrugged his scrawny shoulders.

"Well, are you above board?" he elaborated, Jay looked bewildered by the question. "Can we trust you?"

"I have worked for Mr Hobbs for nine years; I have control of his bank accounts and shares. I oversee all of his business accounts and any business deals that are presented to him. Mr Hobbs trusts me."

"But that's not what I asked, can *we* trust you?"

"It depends on what you want to see him for."

"It is not a business deal or anything to do with shares," Vic smiled.

"I see," he looked at them both separately, "let's hear it then."

"Okay," Mason sat forward and explained to Jay what had happened and how far Mark Hobbs was involved. Of course Jay was concerned, this was his boss they were talking about. Would he be in as much danger as the girl? "What we need to establish, sunshine, is if he knows where she is, she needs protecting."

"Mr Hobbs is at his other home in Austin, he has a house down there and I believe your friend stayed with him for a while, look, if the police get involved…"

"Let's hope it doesn't come to that, mate," Mason smiled as a pretty brunette placed a tray of iced tea on the desk in front of them. "Uh, what is this?"

"It's your tea," Jay replied.

"Um, that's got ice and lemons in it, governor," Vic frowned.

"This is the finest iced tea in Texas," Jay explained.

"I don't care where it's from, there is only one way to drink tea and that's with milk and sugar." He replied sourly.

"Leeann can get you sugar and milk if you prefer."

"Is he havin' a giraffe?" Vic groaned, "Are you playing silly buggers, mate?" Jay looked at Mason confused,

"He means that you must be having a laugh at us," Mason explained.

"I can assure you that I am not laughing at either of you, I don't even have a sense of humour, according to my ex-wife."

"You're a funny bloke, mate, I'll give you that," Vic chuckled.

"In England we take our tea hot with milk and sugar," Mason explained. "I would have thought an educated bloke such as your good self would have known that."

"Mark and I are old college buddies, I have never left US soil. I don't travel well, so I stay here and he does the travelling. As for hot tea, I saw that EastEnders program on TV once, I know you drink it hot, but I thought as you both seem to be world wise as it were, that maybe you'd like iced tea on such a hot and sunny day."

"Again with the EastEnders crap," Vic stood, "that program is an insult to the East end, sunshine; you'd do well to remember that in future. Come on, Mason, me old son, we have a long drive ahead of us, if Jay here can oblige us with an address, that is."

"Of course," he swallowed hard, "I am sorry if I offended you." He added handing Mason a piece of paper with an address written on it.

"It's alright, mate, no harm done," Mason smiled and stood, Jay wrote down the address and they walked to the door, "Should anyone else come in here asking questions…"

"I won't tell them anything," he smiled slightly.

"You can't miss 'em," Vic added, "they are even uglier than we are."

"Speak for yourself," Mason chuckled and followed him out.

"That was easy," Vic said pressing the elevator button.

"Mmm, too easy if you ask me," Mason frowned looking at the address on the paper, "Come on, let's just double check," he said marching towards Jay's door.

He opened it and Jay was out on the balcony talking on his phone.

"No, they didn't say where they were from," he said, "that's right, tall, big, English with cockney accents."

"You forgot to say gorgeous, mate," Vic smiled and took hold of Jay's arm. Mason took the phone out of Jay's hand. "So, are we going to have to do an Arnie on you? You know where we just let you go?" he nodded over the balcony railing.

"I was merely notifying Mr Hobbs that you were going to see him," he anxiously explained, "please, I bruise easily."

"If you are lying to us," Vic warned, "you won't need to worry about bruises where you are going," he looked over the edge of the balcony, "there won't be much of you left to scrape up, let alone bruise," he then turned to him. Vic tightened his grip, "So, is this the right address for Mark Hobbs?"

"Ask him, he's on the phone," Jay frowned.

"Hello?" Mason said into the phone.

"Who am I talking to?" the voice demanded.

"Well, sunshine, I can be one of two things, your best mate or your worst nightmare, so what's it gonna be?"

"I am listening," Mark said seriously.

"Right, well, if you are Mark, then you will know what I am talking about, Lisa is in danger. Jock has found out she is dealing with you and he has sent someone over to kill her and most probably you too, mate."

"What address has he given you?" Mark asked him, Mason read it off the paper.

"That's correct, I'll meet you there, it should take you about two hours, Jay will give you directions, I am going to find Lisa."

ᙡᙡᙡ

Mark hung up the phone and rubbed his hand over the sweat that had formed on his forehead. He wasn't afraid for his life, only afraid of losing her. He dialled her cell, but got no answer. She was fine when he left her only a few hours ago, had they got to her already, would he find her body in the house?

He raced over to the college and found Ethan sat talking to some girls on the grass outside, he ran up to him and gave a stern tug on his arm, he followed Mark to his car,

"Where is Lisa?" he demanded.

"She's at home, I think?" he frowned, "problem?"

"You could say that, they know where she is."

"Who?" Ethan frowned.

"They, Jock Mackenzie has sent someone to kill her, we have to get her out of here." He didn't need to hear anymore and ran to his car, revving the engine as he stated it he then followed Mark back to the house. But Lisa wasn't there.

She still didn't answer her cell phone and had left no word as to where she was going to be. Why would she, she had stupidly trusted the fact that no one had found her yet. She believed that she was safe.

She sat in the sun at the park trying to work out in her head what she could do about Mark. She picked at the muffin she had bought and sipped her water. The sun felt warm and she was wondering if there could ever be something between her and Mark. He was extremely handsome, single; perhaps interested in her, baby or no baby, she would never need worry about another thing again. She contemplated what sort of life they would have and if they would ever be safe away from Jock. Then it hit her heart hard, Jock would never give up as long as he thought she had the diamonds, he'd never leave her alone. Her phone buzzed again, it was Ethan this time, she couldn't seem to get a moments peace.

"Yes?" she snapped.

"Come home, they know where you are," he said, she snapped the phone shut and jumped to her feet.

How did they find out where she was? Her stomach swirled as she trotted back to the car, she started the engine and almost reversed into another car before driving like a maniac back to the house.

Mark and Ethan jumped to their feet as she slammed the front door shut, throwing her bag on the floor and tossing her keys on the phone table,

"How?" she demanded. "How do they know, Mark?"

"I think one of my contacts may have leaked that I had stones to see and he put two and two together," he explained. "It's alright, I have a private jet we can go anywhere you want."

"Who told you?" she frowned.

"Two men from London called me from my office, they tried to say they were here to protect you. I gave them the wrong address to delay them, so it's up to you."

"Oh, my God, I can't fly in this condition," she frowned and rubbed her quivering hand over her tummy.

"Lots of pregnant women fly all the time, Lisa," Mark snapped, it took her aback briefly, but there was no point in her being Holly anymore. "We have to go, so you need to pack some things in a bag and any cash you have lying around, they cannot find you here."

"How will they?" Ethan asked feeling sick with fear.

"Well, you two haven't exactly hid your wealth now, have you? It wouldn't take them long to ask a few questions to find out where you are," Mark explained.

"You called me Lisa," she sighed slightly dismissive of the situation.

"Until we sort you out another identity, I think you should both go back to your real names. Saves confusion," Mark replied. "Please, we need to hurry," Rory pulled Lisa up the stairs, they packed their clothes and Lisa emptied the safe in her closet of the thousands of dollars she had hid there just in case, for this precise moment. She loaded them into a duffle bag and then she joined Rory and Mark in the hall, they ran to the door, "Right, so do we fly or drive?" Mark asked opening the door.

"Fly," Rory said, "it's faster."

"Drive," Lisa added, "it's safer for the baby."

"If we drive, Lisa, there might not be a baby," Rory snapped harshly.

"So let's split up then," she said. "I'll drive and you two can fly."

"No, we go together and we're wasting time," Mark opened the door and they ran to his car, he loaded the bags in the back and revved the engine as they snapped in their seatbelts.

"I am going to miss this place," Rory sighed as Mark drove them down the drive.

"You'll be able to come back, we just need to hide you for a few months, Jock will get tired of chasing you." Mark explained. Lisa knew Jock would never give up, not until either he had the diamonds back or she was dead, but more probable than anything, both.

Once on the highway Mark's phone rang, he answered it on speaker phone and they all listened,

"So, mate," Mason said, "where the 'ell are ya?"

"Change of plans," he frowned, "I'm sorry, guys, but I can't trust you on this."

"Look, sonny Jim, we have put our arses on the line to protect the girl are you telling me we have wasted our time coming here, there are right behind us," he groaned.

"I don't even know your name," Mark shrugged.

"Mason, the girl will know us, know that we mean her no harm, we just want to protect her," he continued. "Tell her I am sorry about Ben, that the others did a number on him, not us," Lisa frowned, it was the other two from the docks in Poole. She remembered them now and how they did seem to want to resolve this without trouble. But could she trust them? "Look, mate, the blokes he's sent after her are hit men, they will kill her and that Irish twat she's with."

"Who are you calling a twat, you cockney eegiate?" Rory snapped.

"So, they are with you," Mason sighed, "Lisa, love you remember us, me and Vic, gentle giants. Just get somewhere safe; we'll call tomorrow when you are off the grid."

"If I can trust you, Mason, you'll get rid of those hit men," Mark added.

"If we get rid of them, we'll get the gas chamber," he replied, "and I am sorry, but no bird is worth the death penalty," Lisa smiled slightly. "We'll be in touch," he then hung up the phone.

They joined the I10 just before eight and then Mark pulled into a motel just outside of El Paso, Lisa was exhausted and Mark felt that they would be safe enough to rest for a few hours. He paid for two rooms, he shared with Rory and Lisa had a room to herself.

She lay on the bed and rubbed her hand over her tummy, concerned now for her unborn child more than anything. A life on the run would never be any sort of life for a baby. But this wasn't just any baby, this was Ben's baby and she couldn't have destroyed it to save herself. She glared at the bag of money as is sat on the bed opposite her.

If she were alone in all of this, she could hide better, disappear again. If neither Mark nor Rory knew where to find her then they would be better off.

She changed her clothes and waited until the lights in the room next door went off. She left most of her clothes in the bags on the bed and crept down the stairs. With her duffle bag on her back she ran up the highway to a truck stop. She asked the waitress if she trusted any of the drivers,

"Stan is your best bet, honey," she smiled, "he'll take you as far as Vegas if you want it."

"Could you please…?" she smiled politely.

"You sit tight and I'll ask him for you," she nodded her head and walked towards Stan, a white hair and bearded man wearing a red baseball cap, he smiled at her and nodded his head, he then stood from his table and pulled some money out of his pocket placed on the table, he walked over to her.

"I am leaving in about ten, is that alright?"

"I can pay you," she offered.

"I wouldn't take a penny off you, sweetie," he smiled.

They were on the road heading north before the sun began to rise, for the first time in months she felt slightly relieved, no one from her old life to remind how much of a mess her current life actually was. She closed her eyes after seeing signs for Roswell, up until then, she had always thought it was just something used in the X-Files. She never believed it was an actual real town in New Mexico.

"Lisa," Rory called quietly while he tapped on the door to her room, "I have tea for you." Mark came out on to the porch, "She must be tired, I think she's still asleep."

"Lisa?" Mark knocked on the door, he shook his head and opened the door, on the bed sat her bags, but she was nowhere to be seen. "She's gone," he frowned.

"What?" Rory stepped into the room, "You don't think they took her, do you?"

"We would have heard, nope, she must have decided to go it alone." He replied wryly.

"Shit," Rory sighed and launched the cup of tea over the railing. It exploded onto the ground, the tea bag burst open. "We have to find her."

"How, did she ever say where she would go if…?"

"No, never," he answered feeling sick.

"Well, she could be anywhere; any trucker in his right mind would pick her up off the side of the road." He marched towards her bags and lifted them, "She only has a day's worth of clothes with her, so let's hit the road and pray we get lucky."

ѿѿѿ

Mason and Vic sat in the car on the street outside
Lisa's house, admiring her taste in both property and
cars.

"I'll give her this much, she has taste," Vic stated.

"Maybe they left something behind to give us a
clue."

"What's the sentence here for breaking into a
house?" Vic asked.

"In this country, most likely death, if you take a
piss on the street, death, if you nick a dog, death, if you
kill someone, it's death," Mason smiled, "but I don't give
a shit, let's go an' have a look," Vic agreed and they
climbed out of the car and began walking around the
huge house. Mason opened the gate at the side, the pool
sparkled in the sun light.

"Flamin' 'eck," Vic smiled, "would you cop a
butchers at that."

"I know," Mason nodded his head, "come on,"
they walked to the patio doors, "It would be too easy if
they were unlocked," he frowned and slid the door
across, "but it appears they left in too much of a hurry to

check," they stepped through the door. Gazing around at the beautiful home Lisa had created, the carpets were thick under their feet and the furniture smelled new, Vic lifted a banana out of the fruit bowl, "Oi, put it back," Mason ordered.

"My guts are knockin'," he groaned and peeled back the skin, before taking a huge bite, Mason shook his head, "What, it will go off by tomorrow," he said with his mouth full.

"I want to get out of here before the 'Old Bill' turn up, so, can we stop nicking the grub and get a move on?"

They continued searching and walked up the stairs, drifting silently from room to room. Vic found Mason standing still in the room at the back of the house, piled high with a crib, teddy bears and baby clothes. He shook his head,

"She's up the duff," he sighed.

"What?"

"She's preggers, mate, got a bun in the oven, Lisa is with child." He elaborated.

"Shit," he frowned, "so, if Jock gets his filthy 'ands on 'er, he'll be killin' the kid an all," Mason pulled out his phone and dialled Mark's number,

"Hello?" Mark said quietly.

"Mark, its Mason, I need to know summink, is she pregnant?"

"Yes," Mark sighed, "we tried to get her to get rid of it, but she wouldn't, its Ben's baby and she won't destroy the only thing she has left of him."

"Put 'er on the phone," Mason snapped.

"I can't."

"Why?" Mason demanded.

"She's not here, she ran away last night, we have no clue as to her whereabouts." He replied.

"You know what, mate, for someone who runs is own business, when it comes to protection, you are bollocks."

"And what is bollocks?" Mark asked giving a sideways glance to Rory.

"Crap, shit, the male organs, you understand now, you plank?" Mason hung up the phone, "Vic, I hate to admit it, but we're fucked, me old son."

"So what do we do now?" Vic asked as Mason's phone began to ring, he shook his head and answered it,

"Mason, why are you insulting me?" Mark demanded, "I can't help it if she ran off, can I? I want to find her as much as you do."

"Where are you?"

"At a motel on the I10, just outside of El Paso," he explained.

"How long will it take me to find you?" he asked.

"Couple of hours," Mark answered.

"Right, sit tight, son, we are on our way," he hung up the phone. "Get your cowboy hat out, Vic, we're going to the Wild West," he smiled slightly and they began to walk down the stairs. Someone tried to open the front door. Mason pushed Vic against the wall holding his finger up to his lips. They crept down the stairs and they could hear someone the other side of the door talking on the phone.

"Nah, it's all locked up, they haven't been here since yesterday," he said, it was one of Jock's boys. "Alright, we'll ask around town, someone is bound to know something." After some time they had left, Mason and Vic left by the same way they came in and ran across the grass to the car.

# Thirteen

"Hello, Nan," Lisa sighed, "it's me."

"Lisa, darling, are you alright?" she loved hearing the sound of her grandmother's voice, it pulled emotion to her throat.

"No, no, I'm scared, Nan and I don't know what to do." She sniffed.

"Tell me what's going on, love," she said softly.

"Ben is dead, I'm in America and they are looking for me."

"Who, love?" Nan pressed.

"His name is Jock Mackenzie, Ben stole some diamonds from him…" her eyes filled with tears again, "the buyer only took half and I am stuck here with all these stones and some hit men are trying to find me to kill me…" she sobbed. "Oh, Nan, I don't know what to do."

"It's alright, sweetheart, if you want me to help you, then you need to tell me everything, Lisa, the whole story, love, alright?"

"Okay," she sniffed.

She started at the night Ben walked into their London loft with a bag of gems ready to be cleaned and finished at leaving Mark and Rory at the motel and hitching a ride to Vegas. She was now pregnant and petrified.

Her Nan listened to her story and knew the only thing she could do was to send someone out to help her, her brother Eddie Riggler and he made her look like an Angel.

ʊʊʊ

Nan called Eddie even though it was three fifteen in the morning, even though he didn't like to be woken unless it was urgent. Well, she considered this to be extremely urgent, vital, in fact, no one threatens to hurt her granddaughter and gets away with it. She dialled his number,

"You better be dead or dying, Enid," Eddie groaned.

"What a way to talk to your little sister, Eddie? Now get out of bed, we need to talk."

"So, it can't wait 'til…I don't know, the ruddy sun is up?" he spat.

"No, it can't."

"Right, I am up," he frowned.

"Eddie, turn the light off," Maggie, his wife moaned.

"See, you woke Maggie up now and you know what she does when she don't get enough kip? She makes my life a misery" he groaned leaving his bed and closing the door behind him.

"Eddie, please, I am sorry your wife wears the trousers in your house, but I really need your help."

"Alright, Enid, I am out of the bedroom and in the lounge, what the hell has got you so upset that you had to call me at this hour?"

"It's Lisa, Jennie's Lisa, she's in trouble."

"What, is she up the duff?"

"Yes," she sighed.

"And you want me to sort the little runt out?" he frowned.

"No, he's dead."

"Stop speaking in riddles, love, tell me what's goin' on," he insisted.

"Can you come down?" she asked.

"What, to Bournemouth, are you mad?"

"No, it would just be easier to talk to you if you were here."

"Listen, love, you have my undivided attention, now spill."


Enid explained the situation to Eddie, he was shocked to discover that his little niece was in fact mixed up with t little known tyke Ben Marshall, even in Croydon he was known for sly dealings and under cutting his customers. But when the name Jock Mackenzie came out something inside this man twitched. He'd known him for years, he use to box with him at the gym he ran for twenty years in the East End that was until Jock took up illegal fist fights and started getting too gobby for his liking. He knew this arrogant, obnoxious bloke and the thought that he wanted to hurt Lisa left a bad taste in his mouth. He killed the boy; the debt was paid as far as he was concerned.

ΩΩΩ

Lisa had already paid for the ticket to bring her uncle Eddie out to her in Vegas. She sat in the arrivals lounge watching everyone, people coming off planes, dressed in wacky clothes, the cabin crew in the perfect matching uniforms and glossy tans, bright white smiles and a chirpy, bouncy walk, business men arriving for a weekend of blowing more than a third of their pay, just because they can. But she was also looking for anyone who might appear a threat to her, Uncle Eddie's flight was due and the screen flashed to say it had landed, all she had to do now was look for him. She remembered his visits when she was a kid, he was over six feet tall with blond hair, light blue eyes and smoked cigars, he had a charismatic smile and an infectious laugh to go with his one liners.

It had been years since she saw him last, but as soon as she did, she knew it was him. He wore a dark brown suit and over his arm draped a beige rain coat, only her uncle Eddie would bring a coat to the Nevada desert. His hair was now silver, what he had left of it, he was more or less bald with it cut short around his ears. On his face he wore his dark brown framed glasses, as soon as he saw her, he smiled, he recognised her because she looked so much like her mum.

"Lisa," he said opening his arms, she dove in and held him tightly.

"Thanks for coming, Uncle Eddie."

"I am not here to judge, love, your Nana has explained everything, now please tell me we can get a decent cuppa in this place?"

"I found a diner that sells Twining's," she smiled, "Where are your bags?"

"Right here, love. I didn't pack a case, no sodding airport is going to lose my grundies, that I will promise you," on his shoulder he had a small bag; he obviously hadn't planned on staying long.

She drove him in the rental car towards the diner, Eddie knew Vegas well, he had been there for many boxing promotions and big rumbles, as he liked to call them. He had trained so many fighters over the years and he got to travel with them. So Vegas and the heat were nothing new, he explained this as she drove,

"If you knew what the weather is like, why bring the coat?" she asked.

"You never know what you might need it for," he winked. He hadn't changed at all and it was nice to have family there with her, "Enid, your mum and brother are at home, I tried to get them to stay with Maggie, but you know what your nan is like, so I got a couple of the boys down there just in case. Can I ask why Jock, Lisa?"

"It was Ben…" she frowned and rubbed her hand over her belly.

"So, how much was this worth to you?" he asked.

"Twenty?"

"Twenty grand?" he frowned.

"No, twenty million, in US dollars," she corrected.

"Those gems must be quite something," he smiled wryly.

"There are a lot and I still have half of them left, the buyer fell through at the last minute."

"Do you have them with you?"

"No, they are in a safe," she explained taking the exit and into the parking lot of the diner.

"Keep them there, Jock is going to want them back above and beyond anything else, he will do what he has to." He told her.

"That's what's scaring me," she admitted rubbing her hand over the bump again.

"When is it due?" he asked.

"Um...uh Christmas," she replied.

"Well, let's go and get a cuppa," he smiled and climbed out of the car. She looked tired and scared, "You really need to look after yourself, darlin', you look knackered."

"I haven't slept well in weeks," she admitted.

"Have you got a Quack to look after ya?"

"I did back in Austin, I really liked it there," she frowned and opened the door to the diner, the cool air con blew in their faces. They were seated near the window, the place was pretty quiet and the cars roaring up the highway outside were the main noise they could hear. She ordered two pots of tea and two blueberry muffins.

"I don't eat any of that foreign muck," he moaned as the waitress put the muffins on the table.

"Uncle Eddie, they're just like Nan's cakes," she smiled, "try one."


After tea and a second round of muffins, as Eddie liked them very much after all, he just stared at her, messed up and tired with a baby growing in her belly. Out of all his nephews and nieces he thought Lisa would have been the one to go far. Obviously she did, she was three thousand miles away from home, but not the way he imagined. He thought she would have worked in the city, jetting all over the world. Instead she got herself mixed up in this mess with one of London's biggest gangsters, an army of heavies out for her blood. On top of all of that she was pregnant and the little runt who got her up the duff was stone cold in some morgue in Jersey.

She drove him to her motel and they checked him into the room next door. He gazed around the room,

"It's not the best," she admitted, "I just thought it would be a little more conspicuous under the circumstances."

"Its fine, treacle and no Maggie to keep me up snoring all night," he smiled. "I'll take a shower and then we can catch up some more."

"I am right next door," she said.

"Alright, love and don't worry, Uncle Eddie is here now," she smiled and left him to it.


As she closed her door her phone buzzed in her pocket, forgetting she was in hiding, she just answered it.

"Lisa," Mark said frantically, "where are you?"

"Mark, I'm okay," she insisted.

"Yes, well, for how long though, come on, tell me where you are I…I miss you," he stammered, a smile crept over her face.

She thought for a few seconds, "I'm at the motel Del A Rosa, its off the interstate near the airport, but I am not alone."

"They found you?" he groaned, his heart sped up in his chest.

"No, I called in some reinforcements," she replied modestly, "my uncle, he's…well, let's just say he makes Jock Mackenzie look like a choir boy."

"Great, uh, I have someone here who wants to talk to you. Don't freak out, just listen to what he has to say, okay?"

"Okay," she sighed.

"Hello, Lisa," Mason said, "how are ya, love?" he asked.

"Still alive," she stiffened.

"Glad to hear it, look, we haven't come to hurt you. I don't care about the gems, I just don't want that arsehole to touch one hair on your head."

"What if you just want to get near me and…?" she asked.

"I have a daughter your age and if she were in trouble and knocked up, I would like to think that someone would help her if she needed it. You can trust us and if you let us help you, I promise you will never see us again," he sounded sincere,

"Alright," she muttered, "but I have my uncle here too."

"Is he all right?"

"He can handle himself," she smiled proudly. "You might have heard of him, Eddie Riggler."

"Eddie Riggler, now that's a name I haven't heard in years, love," he smiled. "Well, they won't know what's hit 'em, that's for certain."

"How…how many?" she asked anxiously, almost too afraid to know the answer.

"Two, well, two came to your house."

"My house," she gasped. "Look, Mark knows where I am, my uncle wants as much help as he can get, so please come and I swear if you help me I will make it worth your while."

"No need, sweetheart, see you soon," the phone went click.


She changed her clothes and went down the stairs to see if they had some more rooms, she booked them all in and then returned to hers, her uncle sat on her bed.

"Don't ever leave your door unlocked again," he snapped, she frowned. "Sorry, treacle, it's just you are too trusting. What if I was one of them? You'd be dead by now."

"Okay, sorry," she grumbled. "We have help coming," she explained.

"The more the merrier," he smiled.

They waited in her room all day, he flicked through the channels on the cable TV and found EastEnders on BBC USA. Eddie was miffed as to how it had made it on TV across the pond. She sat anxiously gazing out of the window at every car that drove passed or stopped in the car park. She missed Rory, that was for sure, but it was nice having her uncle there. He was home for her, though she missed her mum and nan implicitly, Uncle Eddie gave her a good substitute.

Time was ticking by, it was almost lunch time and as she considered leaving the motel to get some food, slamming car doors caught her attention.

"They're here," she announced jumping to her feet.

"Come on then, let's go and be friendly," he stood from the bed.

"About Mark, he's really nice and I like him a lot, so, please don't scare him off."

"Would I?" he grinned.

He followed her down to the car, before she could say anything Mark dived into her arms,

"You scared the hell out of me," Mark said into her ear, she liked the warmth it gave her, "Don't ever do that to me again."

"I thought I was protecting you," she muttered.

"If something happened to you, I don't know what I'll do," he exclaimed, he held her back from his chest and glanced over her, "Well, you look alright."

"I am a big girl, Mark," she pouted leaving his embrace and feeling suddenly cold.

"I know…I uh, I believe you know Mason and Victor."

"Vic," he corrected, he hated being called Victor.

"Of course," she smiled slightly, "uh, this is my Uncle Eddie."

"Nice to meet you, Uncle Eddie," Mark said holding out his hand. Uncle Eddie shook his hand and nodded.

"Eddie Riggler," Mason marvelled, "I haven't heard anything about you in years, mate."

"That's because when the world is full of Muppets, it's time to retire," Eddie replied. "I think we should get inside."

They followed Lisa inside and continued the niceties once locked safely in her room. Rory hadn't said a word to her, he still felt cheated by her, deserted. He gave up his life to ensure she was safe out of honour to his friend, the second it got a little heated, she ran off leaving him behind.

She ordered food and while they waited Rory went out on her balcony for a cigarette.

"I thought you had given up," she said from behind.

"Well, my so called friend went AWOL on me, so I feel it's justified," he snapped.

"I had to think of the baby," she muttered.

"The baby is safe inside of you, but if you get shot…" he began, too upset to finish the sentence.

"I know," she frowned.

"Sill, coming here is a good place to hide I suppose, you can practically lose yourself in Vegas," she smiled slightly and nodded. "I was so scared, Lisa. I thought they had got you."

"I am sorry, Rory."

"I have decided that I am sticking with Ethan, never did care for Rory," he smiled.

"Ethan it is then." She nodded.


When they returned to the others, they were discussing a plan to lure the other two heavies to Vegas, to eradicate them once and for all. Eddie suggested heading back to Austin, to attack them on Mark's home ground. But Lisa hoped to be able to return to her house one day and if she allowed a war to break out, she doubted she'd be able to go back there ever again. Mark and *Ethan* decided that it would be better to confront them in Vegas, neutral turf.

Mark contacted Jay and informed him to let everyone know that he was in Vegas. Mason contacted Julian and told him to somehow let it slip that he and Vic had taken a sudden trip to Vegas on business. Hoping that Jock would put two and two together and come up with six.

Waiting for Julian to call back to warn them that Jock knew where they were, was painful. Lisa wasn't as scared as she was before, not with five men to look after her, she didn't feel so alone. She thought how Ben would have loved it, all of this attention and to be among some ruthless men that had a wealth of experience. He used to talk about the boys from Poplar all of the time and now she was sat with three of them.

Mark seemed unusually quiet and it unnerved her slightly, he was normally so outgoing and talkative, not liking awkward silences he would find something to use to strike up a conversation, but as the hours of the day wound down he seemed increasingly agitated. She watched as he received a text message, the colour drained away from his face and sweat formed above his top lip. He anxiously rubbed his hand over his face and stood.

"I need to make a call," he said and left the room. Mason looked at Vic and Ethan who were now playing cards. Eddie didn't miss a trick, he and Mason walked out onto the balcony and gazed over at Mark as he stood by his truck talking angrily into his phone. They couldn't hear what he was saying, but it didn't take Einstein to work out that it wasn't good. He glanced up and saw them watching, turned his back on them and quickly ended the call.

When he returned to the room, he was sweating profusely and looked sicker than a dog. "Damn ex-wife," he groaned.

"You have an ex-wife?" Lisa frowned.

"Yes, major bitch and that's why she's my ex-wife." He replied bluntly and walked out onto the balcony. "She's trying to take me to court," he said to Mason and Eddie, "Wants more alimony, as if twenty grand a month isn't enough," he scoffed. "Women, I made that mistake once and never again," he added.

Lisa stood quietly from the bed and left the room. Mark certainly wasn't the man she thought he was. She wondered if he had ex's, of course he did, he was drop dead gorgeous. The décor of his house was far too nice to be the design of a man, but she didn't like to hear him talk as if he were done with women, especially since she was toying with feelings that had slowly developed for him over the past few weeks.

She hovered on the cool landing hiding from them and fighting to get her emotions under control. The door opened and she snapped her head up, Mark stood humbly in the doorway,

"I was thinking about going for some food, you all must be hungry," she blurted.

"I'm sorry I didn't tell you about Reagan," he muttered. She frowned. "My ex-wife," he added.

"Its fine," she shrugged, "nothing to do with me, is it?"

"Of course it is, I like you and I was wrong to drop this on you like that." He raised his hand and gently caressed her arm. "What if I come with you to get the food and then I can tell you all about the biggest mistake I ever made."

"Okay," she nodded and went inside the room to collect her bag. She told them where she was going and that Mark was going with her.

She drove them towards the diner she had taken her uncle to, hoping they did take away meals and that she could get some beer for them all to help relax them slightly. The tension in the room was so high, a naked flame would cause them all to combust.

"I have to ask you something," Mark stated and turned in his seat to face her. "Is there ever going to be an 'Us'? I mean, I really like you, Lisa and I have been wondering about the chemistry between us, is it real or am I imagining it?"

Her cheeks flushed pink, "I do like you," she admitted, "but, with everything that's going on, I can't think straight, let alone consider the possibility that there could be something between us."

He sat silent for a few moments, "Well, as long as I know that there is something, that is better than nothing at all." He said finally.

"Tell me about the real you, I won't tell a soul, but before I can decide about us, I need to know a bit more about you."

"Promise?"

"I promise," she smiled.

"My real name is Eugene Forest, you can see why I changed it." He grinned. She flashed her brown eyes towards him and supressed her smile. "Actually is Eugene Alfred Forest the Third, but we won't go into that. Anyway, I grew up on a ranch in Kansas where I went to school, had a weekend job at Dairy Shack and dated a pretty girl called Mindy. I had a sister called Carolyn and my parents were normal, I suppose. Poppy worked the ranch and Momma kept house. I had a hot meal every night, went to church every Sunday and I did everything I was told to do. When the ranch went into foreclosure, the bank gave my parents three weeks. Desperate, my father went and borrowed a large amount of money from a nasty piece of work, J.D. Hollings. He now owned the ranch and after a few weeks, he decided that we had to go."

"That's awful," Lisa frowned.

"My sister was sixteen at the time, she was just coming into her own, you know. Well, J.D.'s son, Brett offered her lift home from school one night and he raped her, said my family owed him and he could do whatever he wanted. She screamed running into the house, my father went to confront Hollings with the sheriff and it was all denied. Carrie bought charges against Brett and that night they came to our ranch, shot my parents in front of Carrie, raped her again and left her for dead. When I got home, I found them, I should have gone to the police but Carrie begged me not to, she went to bed and I buried my parents in the pasture. When I got up in the morning she had taken a bottle of sleeping pills."

"I am so sorry," she sighed, her eyes filling with tears, no wonder he seemed to guarded. Barely able to concentrate on her driving, he continued.

"I got my dad's shot gun and went over to their mansion. Brett was outside with his friends, I could have shot him there and then, but I waited until his friends left, then I got to thinking that they would pin it all on me, so I went to see the sheriff, he sent some guys over to my house where they found the bodies, just as I had said.

238

They found the paperwork to the loan that my father would never have paid off and that was all the evidence they needed, Brett was charged with rape, his father of extortion and I was placed into the witness protection program, that's when I met Ben."

"Ben told me how he took you to a pub and that you hadn't even drunk a beer, but he only knew you as Mark."

"They sent me to the UK when the trial had finished as it was rumoured that Hollings had put a price on my head. You can understand my reluctance, if the feds knew, I would disappear again."

"So, why are you dealing in dodgy diamonds?" she asked.

"I don't normally, this is a one off. As soon as I heard from Rory about Ben, I almost pulled out, but I made him a promise and I am a man of my word."

"What about Reagan then, how did you meet her?"

"I met her when I started work at her father's company in Houston. Within a year, I was a shareholder and now I own it. He died and left it all to me, the whole company, go figure. Anyway, she and I got engage within a few weeks of meeting and she rushed the wedding because she was already knocked up with some other guy's baby."

"How did you know that it wasn't yours?" she asked.

"I hadn't slept with her yet. I was still a virgin and don't pretend you are surprised, with a name like Eugene and a healthy church attendance record, abstinence was all in when I was in high school." He smiled. "On our wedding night, she confessed after we had slept together for the first time. I had the marriage annulled, I couldn't be married to someone like that, so she's my ex-wife, but we're not divorced, we're free agents, her mother has disowned her and I agreed to give her twenty grand a month to help with the kid and all." He explained wryly.

"So, even though the baby isn't yours, you agreed to pay her money anyway?"

"Yes, I guess I am a sucker for a hard luck story." He nodded with a shrug. "She's so spoiled though, there is no way she'd get out there and find a real job." Lisa stopped at the diner and they climbed out. "So, now you know all of my dirty, little secrets. What are yours?"

"I am practically a saint, you know," she gleamed a grin, her eyes sparkled in the sunlight and her motherly glow made her all the more attractive.

"I did wonder what the halo was all about," he chuckled as they entered the diner.

# Fourteen

After some food they all felt a little better, Lisa more so. It took a lot for Mark to tell her about his life and for that she felt extremely special and privileged. Mark felt good that he managed to get a lot off his chest. Having an ex-wife could have ruined his chances with Lisa and now he hoped that because he had confided in her, perhaps she would realize just how much she meant to him. Though the phone call had nothing to do with his ex-wife, he hadn't heard from her in months.

The sun set and the day wound down, drinking cool beers and enjoying the stories of the good old days from them all, lightened the atmosphere somewhat and they were all able to relax. Jet lagged and tired, they began to go to bed. Uncle Eddie went to his room, leaving just Lisa and Mark up. Lisa gazed over the busy highway as the orange sun disappeared behind a line of dark blue clouds.

"It's gorgeous out here tonight," Mark said quietly from her side. The sound of his voice startled her slightly. "Sorry, do you want to be alone?"

"No, its fine," she smiled and turned to face him. "Thank you for being honest with me, Mark. After everything I have been through, it means a lot to know there is someone out there that I can trust." He pursed his lips, he wasn't honest with her and if he had been, she would never have anything to do with him again. He had to do this, he had to gain her trust and use it against her, that was the deal and he had no way out of it, no matter what it would do to him or her for that matter, he had no choice. "Was that too much?" she asked.

"No, it just surprised me is all." He lied and swallowed hard.

"When this is all over, if you still like me, and want me, then maybe we can go on a date or something. Isn't that what you Americans call it?"

"Yes," he smiled. "What do the English call it?"

"I don't know, Ben asked me out and I said yes," she shrugged.

"So, I would just say what, Lisa will you go out with me?"

An nervous smile crept across her face, "Yes," she blushed.

"Thanks for the input; I'll know what to do when the time comes." He smirked and crossed his arms over his chest, "Are you planning on staying over here then?" he asked.

"Yes, I love it here, I have that house too, that house is more than the loft I lived in back in London." She babbled, "Then there's you," she added.

"I am happy to hear that," he nodded.

"That's something then," she blurted, "I better go to bed before I do and say something really stupid."

"Something like?"

She smiled crookedly and bit her bottom lip, "I uh," she walked towards him, "I just..." she moved her hands around his neck, with her heart pounding her chest, she gazed at his perfect lips, her mouth watered at the aroma of his aftershave, she leaned in slowly and pressed her lips to his. He folded his arms around her waist and pulled her into his body. It was all he had hoped it to be, her sweet lips made his tongue tingle. As she pulled away, she smiled. "Goodnight, Mark."

He cleared his throat, still tasting her on his tongue, "Goodnight, Lisa."

As he drifted back to his room he pulled his cell from his pocket and pressed dial. "Hello?"

"The deal is off, I am not doing it." He stated.

"Tough titties, laddie, you don't have a choice." The line clicked, he tightened his phone and squeezed his hand.

She climbed into bed and pulled the covers over her body. Though outside it was almost eighty, inside the air con had kicked in and goose bumps covered her body. She smiled as she closed her eyes, Mark was certainly someone she could see herself spending a lot of time with.

Soft knocking on the door disturbed her dreamless sleep. As she pulled the door open Rory smiled humbly,

"What's the matter?" she asked.

"Apparently Mark had a call from his office, he has set up a meeting with the two Muppets Jock has sent here and he and Uncle Eddie have gone to meet them."

"You are joking," she shook her head and pain shot through her body.

"No, Mason and Vic are thinking about going after them, but Mark made me promise to keep you safe here."

"Let me get dressed and we can sort something out, I am not staying here with my uncle and my boy…uh, I mean, my friend out there with God knows who, no bloody way."

"Are you and Mark…?" he frowned.

"Um, not exactly," she couldn't disguise her blush. "We kissed, last night for the first time, it's nothing really."

"Your face and that smile tells me it's a lot more than nothing, Lisa." She said nothing and closed the door.

She met Mason and Vic in Rory's room, he had shared with Mark and she couldn't help but smile at

Mark's neatly made bed. Rory noticed and smiled at her as she stood there gazing off into her day dream.

Rory explained as they waited that Mark told him to sit tight, but all they wanted to do was head off out to find them. Uncle Eddie was not an idiot, he would not allow Jock's boys to get the better of him, but Lisa still worried about her uncle and her soon to be boyfriend. What if they had guns? What if they took them captive and wanted the diamonds from her to get them free?

Three long and agonizing hours passed and not a word from either of them. Wherever they had arranged to meet them, they were late back. Mason tried Mark's office, but it was Saturday and as he suspected, no one was there. Vic called Julian to see if he knew anything, but his phone went straight to voicemail.

Things were beginning to look grim and Lisa was about to give up when Mark's car came whizzing around the block and screeched to a stop outside of the motel.

He stumbled through the door, the side of his white shirt was covered in blood, his face was smashed up and he couldn't even see out of one eye. His hands shook violently as he sat on the bed.

"Oh, my God, what the hell happened?" Lisa screeched.

"I'm sorry, I tried everything, I offered to give them everything I had, but they wouldn't back off."

"Who?" Mason snarled.

"Two very large men in black suits and a black BMW. They looked like something out of the freaking Matrix." He frowned. "They threatened to kill Jay if I didn't agree to meet them. Eddie insisted he come with me," he turned to Lisa. "I am so sorry, honey, so sorry. But he made me come back, he made me come and tell you."

"Where is he?" she asked weakly.

"I'm sorry." He muttered as he stood to walk towards her.

"Mark, where the hell is my bloody uncle?" she demanded angrily.

"He told me to get back to you, to leave them to him, he'd sort them out," he explained sitting back on the bed. Ethan handed him a towel and he wiped the blood from the side of his face. "He's on the highway in Death Valley. There are some mountains nearby and a huge tree at the thirty-one mile marker." He reached out his hand to her, "I am sorry, baby, he made me leave him."

"We should go," Vic said standing from the chair hooking Mason's golf clubs over his shoulder.

"Lisa, love," Mason frowned, "do you have a map?"

"I'll buy one," she stated lifting her bag, all four of them looked at her. "I am not staying here, my uncle came here to help me, I am not leaving him out there alone."

"Why don't you wait with me?" Mark asked.

"No, Rory, I mean, Ethan, will wait with you, I need to go, I'll be alright with these two." She insisted.

"Lisa, I am sorry," Mark admitted.

"You shouldn't have left him, he'd never do that to you." She scorned and left the room.

# Fifteen

After stopping for gas, bottles of water and a map, she returned to the car. Both Mason and Vic waited patiently, not understanding Mark's actions for one second. It just seemed strange that he would leave a man in his seventies to a pair of thugs. Neither of them wanted to say out loud what they thought, but she could tell that they were pretty cheesed off and the banter between them had stopped completely.

She started the engine and slipped the shifter into gear. Mason opened the map once they hit the highway and rested it on his lap. Death Valley was huge, the words needle and haystack fluttered around his head. He gazed out of the window at the never ending cracked, desert surface. The bright blue sky and white sun reflected off the ground and burned at his eyes as he tried to focus.

Vic's cell phone lost signal about a mile away from where Mark had said he left Eddie. When they got to mile marker thirty-one, no one was to be seen.

The tire tracks in the gravel at the side of the road were fresh and there was a lot of blood. Her heart stopped as she gazed at the patch of dried blood on the white road. The hot sun burned down from above and ripples of heat distorted the horizon as they gazed around not knowing what to do.

Vic lifted his phone out of his pocket, "I'm gonna go up on that rock and see if I can get a signal." He said. Pointless really, they were in the middle of nowhere, there certainly weren't any aerials for miles. Still the white rocky sand crackled under his shoes as he walked towards the rock.

Just as he began to climb the rock he heard a groan, but something caught his eye, a black dot on the horizon with a plume of dust shooting from behind it. A car was coming and it seemed likely that it was probably Jock's men.

"Mason," he called out, Mason spun around, "they're coming." Mason took a firm hold on Lisa's hand and pulled her towards the rock. "We need the shooters," Vic added. He let her go and ran back to the car, pulled out his golf bag and dragged it back to Lisa.

"We have to hide," he told her pulling her towards the rock.

"They might have my uncle," she moaned as he towed her. Vic climbed down to look behind the rock,

"Shit!" He roared. "Mason, uh, I found Eddie." He crouched down over Eddie. He was barely conscious, only groaning now and then with blood pouring from the side of his head and more on the side of his body. "It's alright, mate, we found ya."

"Bloody hell," Mason sighed shaking his head.

"Uncle Eddie," Lisa shrieked, "Oh, my God, what happened?"

Eddie opened his eyes slightly, "M-Mark," he muttered.

"He's safe, mate, back at the motel." Mason assured him.

"K-keep him away from Lisa," he then groaned in pain.

"Uncle Eddie," she sniffed.

"I'm alright, love." He said using Vic's hand to sit up, "could use a drink though."

"I'll get the water," Mason said and hurried back to the car. He found the water and turned to run back as a black Mercedes screeched to a stop. "Victor," he called out.

"Stay here," he told Lisa, removed two hand guns from the golf bag, tucked them into the top of his trousers and stood. "Whatever happens, stay here." She nodded and rested her uncle's head on her lap.

Vic joined Mason and sneakily slipped a gun into Mason's hand. Mason placed the bottled water on the ground and stood firm with his friend and partner at his side. Two huge men with wide necks, donning black Ray Ban sunglasses, with white shirts, climbed out of the car, slamming the doors closed in unison. One had hardly any hair at all and the other had dark hair, but cut very short.

"Vic, me old mate," Mason murmured, "I have a bad feeling about this."

"What, just like you get a bad elbow when its gonna rain?"

"Nope," Mason smirked. "Like, we're gonna have to drag their heavy arses through the sodding desert to bury the buggers."

"Yeah, they look like they ate all the pies, mate."

"Don't they just." Mason agreed.

"Well, well, well." The one with the dark hair chuckled. "What do we have here? Victor and Mason, now how the hell did you find your way here?"

"Bloody sat-nav I got from Mohamed on the market, it's a duff, don't trust his gadgets." Mason replied smartly. The other man smiled slightly.

"I did tell him to turn left at the roundabout," Vic added.

"Does Jock know you are here?" the other asked.

"I don't know, can I ask the audience?" Vic joked. Mason grinned.

"Heard you two were a couple of clowns," the first sniped.

"It's his feet," Mason motioned his head towards Vic, "Bloody size fourteen, clown shoes were all we could find for him."

"They're not that big," the other frowned.

"Big enough to kick your arse, son," Vic boasted.

"I don't fight O.A.P's," he snarled.

"Yeah, that's what your mother said last night after I finished shagging her," Vic grinned.

"You cheeky bastard," he charged forward, but his partner stopped him.

"We're here for the tart, not him."

"What tart?" Mason asked, "Your sister?"

"She's here with you, isn't she?" he said looking at the rock, "She's with the old man right now."

"Who are you calling old, son?" Eddie asked stepping out from the rock holding a gun out in front of him.

"Lee, I thought you finished him off," the dark haired bloke groaned angrily.

"I thought I did, Grant, it's not my fault he didn't die," Lee moaned.

"I, my son, am your worst nightmare, I have comeback more times than Freddy bloody Krueger. I make Jason look like a child in a hockey mask. I am the Michael Myers of your own Halloween. You made a mistake coming after my niece, you killed her boyfriend and now you are here to kill her. Well, it's not going to happen."

"And why is that, old man?" Grant asked.

"Two boys such as yourselves could get lost in a place like this. We could bury you from the neck down and leave you to the buzzards. They'd dine for a week on your nose alone, my son. So you have a choice." Eddie moved closer. "Sod off and tell your boss she has disappeared completely or we bury you."

Grant shook his head pulling his gun from behind him and dangling it at his side. "I can't go back without the gems, Mark is getting them for us, but she can't live."

"That's bollocks and you know it," Eddie snapped.

"Jock won't…"

"I don't give a toss what Jock want's, the man is a twat, a complete an utter twat, you can tell him that if you want, or are you going to be bird food?" Eddie barked. Grant lifted his gun and aimed it at Eddie. Eddie aimed his gun at Grant, Vic and Mason aimed their guns at Grant and Lee.

"Well now," Uncle Eddie smiled proudly, "what we have here is a 'Deal or No Deal' kind of situation. In Vic's box, he has forty years of experience and has even been inside for a stint or two. His wife bloody hates him and he couldn't give a monkey's if he never saw the UK again. In the other box is my friend Mason. Another veteran with a wealth of experience, a daughter who has just emptied his bank account after her dream wedding to a Pikey boxer who would tear your arms off and beat you with the soggy end. Then you have me, I'm the banker and I am betting you would prefer a nice fat cheque rather than a shallow grave. So, you can have a million quid between ya, if the pair of you sod off and allow Lisa to disappear. Deal or no deal?"

"No deal. I can't do that grand-dad, can't let her go, Jock wants her head on a plate." Grant smirked. Without even thinking about it, Eddie pulled the trigger of his gun and shot Grant in the knee.

"Aghh!" he groaned falling to the ground.

"Call me a bloody grand-dad." Eddie retorted. "So, now, Lee, are you going to disrespect me too?"

"You are off your rocker, mate, there was no need for that." He shook his head.

"Are you going to try and kill my niece?"

"I haven't got a choice," Lee sighed. Eddie raised his gun, "Alright, just wait, let me…" he turned and looked at the car, dived towards it and hid behind the boot. Eddie raced towards Grant. He aimed his gun up at Eddie as sweat poured from his head. Blood splattered across his white shirt and his hand was shaking. Vic and Mason stood behind Eddie, Vic squeezed his gun in his hand as sweat formed in his palm, Eddie raised the gun in his hand and aimed it at Grant's head.

"Is Jock really worth dying for?" Eddie asked.

"If I go back," he spluttered, "I'm dead anyway. I am going to Hell, mate, and you are coming with me," he squeezed his finger on the trigger, but before it could fire, Eddie shot his gun and the bullet hit Grant in the middle of his forehead. Grant's gun slipped from his hand, landing at Eddie's feet, as he leaned down to get it, Lee started firing at them.

Vic shot first, hitting the roof of the car before diving towards Lisa's parked car, Mason fired a couple of rounds before joining his friend.

Bullets whizzed past Eddie's head, Lee showed his inexperience, he couldn't shoot for shit. Eddie crawled on his hands and knees and hid behind a boulder at the side of the road.

"That was my brother," Lee roared between shots.

"You had a choice," Eddie called over to him from behind the rock.

"You don't get a choice with Jock, you know that."

"Look, son," Eddie called out. "I don't want to kill you, but I will if you don't listen to reason."

Lee stopped firing and stepped out from behind the car. Eddie stood and slowly approached him. Lee looked at his brother's body on the ground, shook his head.

"I didn't want to kill him, son, you got to believe me." Eddie sighed.

"He's only twenty four, never even left London before, and now, now he's dead, my mum is going to kill me."

"When you get mixed up with a nasty bastard like Jock, this is what happens and kids get killed."

"I don't know what I am going to do, Grant always told me what to do..." Lee said shaking his head.

"Why don't you come with us, we'll sort something out."

"I have to wait," he sighed shaking his head again.

Eddie looked at a plume of dust rising rapidly into the blue sky, another car was approaching. "You're not on your own, are ya?"

"Do you think Jock would send us here on our first job alone?"

"You poor kids," Eddie said shaking his head. "Listen, we can get in the car and go before they get here."

"They'll find me," he swallowed. The black BMW M3 screeched to a stop. Lee turned his head and looked at it. For a few moments it just sat there, then the doors opened and before anything else, bullets were firing everywhere again.

Mason and Vic shot at the other two men, dressed in black polo shirts, wearing Ray Bans. Eddie hit the ground as a bullet careered past his head, his gun fell from his hand, sliding away a few feet in front of him on the rubble covered road. He scurried towards it, as the driver of the other car took a bullet to the throat and clutched at his neck, claret squirted from his neck, spraying the car and the ground.

The passenger continued to shoot at Vic and Mason until his gun ran out of ammo. Mason and Vic stepped out from behind the car, firing their guns continuously as they walked towards the passenger who had coward down behind his open door. Both of them towered above him, he had already taken a bullet in his shoulder and blood was pumping out of him. He sat on the ground and gazed up at them. For a few moments Mason wondered if he could let him live, let him go back to Jock. No, there would be repercussions; no one could survive this from Jock's point of view.

"Goodnight, sunshine," Mason grinned and both he and Vic shot him in the head.

Eddie was still scurrying for his gun when Lee stepped on it, Eddie looked up to him.

"An eye for an eye, isn't it?" Lee asked. "You killed my brother, so now I'll kill your niece, after I kill you, that's only fair." His hand was trembling; Eddie could see this was something Lee hadn't done before.

"You don't want to do that..." Eddie began.

"It's the only way...," click, "sorry, Grand-dad...," click, Eddie closed his eyes, thinking about his wife and kids, wondering if they'd ever understand. He never did get around to painting the shed up at his allotment.

The bang echoed out and Eddie honestly thought that Lee had pulled the trigger. Vic and Mason turned from the car and rushed to Eddie's side as Lee collapsed on the ground with a single bullet hole in his forehead. The three of them turned around, Lisa stood holding a smoking gun out in front of her.

# Sixteen

Mason lit a rag hanging from the fuel cap opening, it ignited immediately and the black Mercedes blew it to smithereens. At the same time, Vic did the same to the BMW. Inside were the bodies of Lee and his brother Grant Evens and of the other two men they discovered to be American with US drivers licences in their wallets, one was called Calvin Gates, and the other Jenson Jones. Vic had removed their teeth and hoped the fire would be enough to burn off any finger prints. It was made to look like there had been a gun battle between the two cars and all four perished in the fire, by the time the police investigated this, they would be long gone. It's not something they liked to do, but it had to be done if Lisa was going to get through this.

She hadn't said a single word since she shot Lee, who turned out to be a nineteen year old kid and he apparently still lived at home with his parents. She wondered if she'd ever get over what had just happened as she gazed at the roaring flames.

"Are you alright, sweetheart?" Eddie asked.

"No, I just murdered someone," she frowned.

"You were defending me, protecting me, so, don't give them another thought. If they had killed you, they wouldn't be feeling guilty right now, I can tell you that much." He assured. "We should get back to the hotel, I have a feeling Mark will be waiting on those Muppets."

"What are we going to do with him?" she asked pushing her feelings for him aside.

"I am going to remove his bloody ball's, my love." He smiled slightly. "Come on, let's get out of here before the smoke attracts the 'the filth'."

She sat in the back of the car with Eddie while Mason drove and Vic navigated from the map. She gazed out of the back window at the plume of black smoke bellowing up from the cars and swallowed hard on her dry throat.

She had killed someone and didn't like how that felt. How could she be a good mother to her baby if she couldn't judge people correctly and was a murderer? Life certainly seemed to be one shit pile after another and now she had to deal with more shit, Mark.

Once back at the motel she followed Mason up the stairs. Vic helped her uncle and Mason held her back from her door before opening it.

Ethan was tied to the chair with a screw driver jammed in each of his thighs. His faded blue jeans were red and his mouth was gagged with a rag. Mason hurried towards him,

"Lisa," Ethan groaned as Mason untied his hands.

"This is getting crazy now," she sighed shaking her head and moving towards him. "Did Mark do this?"

"No, Jock's men did it," he replied.

"They were here?" she frowned, suddenly feeling sick again.

"Yes, Mark had made some sort of deal with Jock, they thought you would have bought the diamonds with you. They beat him up pretty bad, Lisa."

"I don't care about him, I am worried about you." She frowned.

"I'm alright, they missed the bones, it's all flesh," he shrugged bravely as Vic proceeded to remove one of the screwdrivers from his leg. Blood spouted and the air was sucked out of the room, Lisa fainted and collapsed on the floor.

"Poor kid," Vic sighed before removing the other screwdriver, "sorry, son, this might hurt a bit," he said giving it a yank. Ethan cried out in pain again,

"Jesus Christ!" He then held the towel over the wounds as Mason told him too.

Vic lifted Lisa from the floor and laid her on the bed, Eddie sat beside her and lifted her hand as she slowly came around. Mason handed her a cup of water, she took it and sipped at it while not taking her eyes off Ethan. He was sweating profusely and the colour had drained from his face, he looked bloody awful.

"Are you alright, love?" Mason asked her.

"We need to get him to a hospital." She groaned sitting up slowly.

"Hospitals ask too many questions, we'll get it sorted when we get back to Texas." Ethan explained. She looked at her uncle.

"Mark is heading there, he has to be," he frowned. She nodded and stood from the bed.

"I need to take my car back first, it's only a rental." She lifted her bag and began filling it with items from around the room. "I'll settle the bill, if you can get Ethan into your car. I'll meet you outside." She said and left them in the room.

She left the car at the Enterprise office and climbed in the back of the car beside her uncle. Feeling wearing and broken hearted she was glad she didn't totally give herself over to Mark. It was just a kiss and she had kissed enough frogs in her time. The only man she could ever trust was dead and Mark was a lesson she wouldn't forget in a hurry.

The drive back to Texas was long and arduous, especially for a pregnant girl. Mason and Vic stopped many times so that they could have breaks and shared the driving, they didn't want to lose any time at all.

Arriving back at her house twenty-two hours later, she kicked off her shoes as they entered the house. She was expecting it to be ransacked, but nothing was out of place and there was no sign that Mark had been anywhere near her home. She told them all to make themselves comfortable and ran up to her room. On her bed there was a note. It was Mark's handwriting and her heart thudded in her chest as she lifted the paper and opened it.

*'Lisa,'*

*'I am so sorry, honey. I had no choice, you have to believe me. Jock has something on me and I couldn't allow him to expose me, I would be dead in a day. Turns out I am a dead man anyway. I know you are okay, I know you are safe because my friend in the FBI is investigating a suspicious fire where the remains of four male bodies have been found in two burned out cars in Death Valley. Your uncle certainly lives up to his reputation. I hope that one day you will find it in your heart to forgive me, and if you can't, I understand. I never meant to hurt you, Lisa, I am in love with you and I have been in love with you since the first day we met. But I suppose that's too late now, take care, honey,*

*Mark.'*

She read it twice before folding the paper up and stuffing it into her pocket. She knew she had read him wrong. She knew he was telling the truth, because it made more sense to believe it than to deny it. Mark did too much for her to be a bad guy and if he was only after the diamonds, he had plenty of opportunities to take them before. This had Jock written all over it and after spending hours in a car with four sweaty men, she had a lot to make him pay for.

When she padded down the stairs she found the men standing around the island in the kitchen. Mason and Vic looked tried,

"Why don't you go and take a shower and nap," she said to them. "You look knackered, we're not going anywhere."

"I could use forty winks," Vic nodded, "are you sure?"

"Yes, now go, I will order us some food and we can all get some rest before we decide what we are going to do next."

After they left the kitchen, she put the kettle on the stove to boil and got an ice cold beer out of the fridge for her uncle. He smiled a thank you after helping Ethan to sit down, then sat on the huge couch in the living room.

"This place is lovely, Lisa," he said and took a swig of his beer.

"I fell in love with the house and I am going to settle here, never again am I going to be ran out of my home."

Ethan frowned and sat beside her on the couch, "What do you mean?"

"I mean I am going back to London to face Jock, I'll give him the rest of the diamonds and then he'll…"

"Kill you," Ethan sighed, "It's not safe, he is not a reasonable man, he is a cold, hard killer and I wouldn't trust him."

"I know, but look," she handed him the note from Mark. "People are getting hurt by protecting me, I am not worth it, Ethan."

"Yes you are, do you know how incredible you are?" he frowned.

"You are my best friend now, Lis, I can't just let you go and do something so bloody stupid." His Irish accent came in loud and clear.

She smiled warmly at the gesture but it hadn't changed her mind, "I don't want to be running for the rest of my life."

"You won't have to if I have anything to do with it," Uncle Eddie groaned. "The Paddy is right, love," he added.

"Who are you calling a Paddy?"

"You, because I can run away and you can't catch me," her uncle winked at Lisa and Ethan chuckled. His legs were still very painful and Lisa decided to try and get him some help.

She left them relaxing on the couch and headed into town. While there she stopped at the bank and removed the diamonds from the deposit box and then headed to her doctors. It was a long shot, but she had to try and get Ethan some help.

She stopped by Dr Munroe's office. Hoping that she could persuade her to come to her house and check

Ethan's wounds, possibly give him some antibiotics to prevent them getting infected.

Dr Munroe was happy to see Lisa who sat anxiously waiting for an appointment. She called her into her office and was instantly concerned by her appearance and apparent preoccupation.

"Is something wrong?" she asked.

"It's not me, okay, it's my uh, my brother." Lisa replied.

"Wow, that accent has come back," she smiled warmly. "Take a seat, I want to check your blood pressure." Lisa nodded and sat on the bed as the doctor checked her over, listened to the baby's heartbeat and confirmed that the baby was fine, though she needed to get some rest. "So, tell me, what's wrong with your brother."

"He had an accident," she answered.

"Okay, take him to the ER across town."

"I…I can't, they'll ask too many questions." Lisa admitted.

"Who will?"

"The police," she frowned.

"What sort of accident did your brother have?" Dr Munroe then asked.

"Uh, he uh, he had screwdrivers rammed into his thighs." The doctor's mouth dropped open.

"Seriously?"

"Yes," she swallowed.

"Do I even want to know what's going on?"

"Honestly, no. It's safer for you if you don't. Listen, I'll understand if you don't want to, but I could really use a doctor's opinion and maybe some antibiotics for him to take."

"I could lose my licence," she shook he head.

"Please, I don't know who else to talk to, they killed Ben, he is the father of this baby and the people who did this are the same people who hurt my brother, if I lose Rory too…I'll pay you, twenty-five grand, please just take a quick look and make sure he isn't going to die on me."

"If I agree, will you tell me all that's been going on?"

"Yes," she nodded finally, realizing this may be the only way to get her help.

"I'll drop by after surgery finishes, okay?"

"Thank you." Lisa smiled relieved and stood.

Dr Munroe peeped over her glasses, "You don't have to pay me, okay? I would just like to know what's going on and see if there is any way I can help you."

"Are you sure? I don't mind."

"I will look at Rory's legs and I won't charge a dime. I'll bring by some meds and then we'll talk, alright?"

"Thank you," Lisa said again and stood from the bed.

When she returned to her house, Rory has developed a high temperature. Uncle Eddie was dousing him down with a cool face cloth and looked very concerned.

"I have a doctor coming to check you over," she said, he could barely open his eyes to acknowledge what she had said. "He can't have an infection already, can he?"

"Depends on how clean those screwdrivers were." Uncle Eddie replied and stood from the couch. He followed her to the kitchen, "A chap called Jay phoned, love, said he needs to speak to you."

"Jay is Mark's assistant," Mason said from behind.

"Do I call him?" she asked unsure of what to do.

"I would see what he has to say," Mason nodded and lifted a cup from the counter, "Mind if I make a drink?"

"No," she shook her head, "help yourself, I have Tetley in that cupboard if you want some English tea."

"Thanks, love, I know Vic would love a proper cuppa." He smiled.

While Mason made some tea, Lisa took her phone out onto the back deck to talk to Jay. She knew it was something to do with Mark and it made her stomach swirl as she wondered what he would do next. Jay asked if he could come over and she agreed as it would be better to see if he was telling the truth if she could actually see his face.

Dr Munroe arrived and Eddie went out to the kitchen while she treated Ethan. Lisa had to remember to call him Ethan now, he had chosen to leave Rory behind. It was easy for him to turn his back on his old life. But she still had ties to her family and was worried sick that as Jock would be able to get to her, they might try and attack her mum and brother, even worse, her frail grandmother.

When she finished dressing his wounds, she came to find them in the kitchen. Lisa made her some coffee and they sat at the counter while Lisa explained everything that had gone on.

Dr Munroe was shocked to hear about the diamonds and of how Ben was beaten to death because of them. She was amazed that Lisa hadn't lost the baby given the situation she was in and all of the stress she was under. Lisa hadn't told her about the dead bodies in the desert that she had helped in putting three.

"I don't condone Ben's actions one bit, Lisa," she said finally. "But I don't judge you either. You made the choice to try and start a new life and I respect that. I sincerely hope you get it all sorted out and the true criminals in all of this are brought to justice."

"Thank you," Lisa mutter as tears formed in her eyes, "Sorry," she sniffed and wiped them with a quivering hand. "I honestly thought we would have got away with it, that Ben and I would have rode off into the sunset and never looked back. The reality is I am stuck here, away from home and my family, I am going to spend the rest of my life looking over my shoulder and for what, money? It is so not worth it, if I could give all of the diamonds back, I would, but I can't and on top of al of that, I have a baby to bring up on my own and I know that's not easy." She sipped her drink, "I remember my mum going without a meal so that my brother and I could eat, she'd go days without food because after all of the bills and clothing for Nick and I, she had nothing left for food. Now I have more money then I need and I wish I could just bring them over and give them a new life, you know?"

"I know, and I expect they would come in a heartbeat," Dr Munroe smiled sympathetically. "Well, I need to go, Rory, or Ethan as he prefers, will be feeling better by the morning." She stood from her chair.

"You won't tell anyone, will you?"

"No," she smiled slightly, "I won't breathe a word, but if I were you, I would try and resolve this, you and the baby need to be able to live and not look over your shoulder for the rest of your life."

"How do I do that?" she frowned.

"Go and see him, on his own turf, call him out on Ben's death. Take witnesses and either get this man in jail or get him away from you forever."

"Thank you, Dr Munroe," Lisa smiled slightly as they walked towards the front door.

"First off, you can call me Shelly," she smiled, "I have known Mark a long time, he is the kindest, most honest man I know. He must have had a good reason to do this to you," Lisa nodded, "Come and see me soon and please try and get some rest."

Lisa watched as she drove away in the golden evening sun. The crickets chirped loudly in the trees surrounding the house and a breeze rustled the branches gently. She inhaled a fragrant breath and went back inside the house.

Vic gave her a lopsided grin as she entered the kitchen, praising her ability to find English tea bags and thanked her for a lovely cuppa. She sat quietly in the living room while she waited for Jay to arrive. She thought a lot about Mark, he had let her down, but she still felt butterflies in her stomach whenever she thought about him and that amazing kiss.

Mason and Eddie sat at the table and talked quietly about where they should go next, agreeing to wait and hear what Jay had to say.

The telephone rang out making them all jump in their seats. Lisa lifted the phone to her ear,

"Hello?"

"It's me," Mark said. "Please wait, don't hang up." She stayed silent while frowning, her uncle stood. "Are you still there?"

"Yes," she muttered and walked out of the living room, "what do you want?"

"To talk, can I come over?"

"I think Mason and Vic are sharpening their pliers to rip your ruddy finger nails out. How could you do that to me?"

"I explained in the letter, I can't be relocated, I just can't." he replied. "So, can we meet up? I need to talk to you."

"No, it's not a good idea," she stiffened.

"Okay, well, you uh, you take care of yourself, you hear?"

"You too," she whispered as her nose tingled and her eyes filled with tears, "good bye,"

"Bye," he replied and the line went dead. She wiped a tear away from her cheek,

"Lisa," her uncle said from behind.

"I uh, I need to lie down," she said and hurried upstairs.

Slamming her door shut she fell onto the bed and sobbed. Allowing Mark in did more damage than she had realized and hearing him say goodbye broke her heart in two.

# Seventeen

Uncle Eddie stood in the hall outside of her door and listened as she cried. It was more than Mark not being who she thought he was. It was weeks of fear and heartbreak, she was still mourning Ben and with Jock trying to kill her, missing her family and worrying about the baby, everything suddenly caved in on top of her and he wondered if she'd ever be alright again.

As he walked down the stairs someone knocked on the front door. He opened the door and found a man in his thirties with very short hair and a nervous disposition.

"Is uh, Holly there please?" he asked.

"Sorry, son, no Holly here," Eddie smiled politely.

"Uh, I am Mark Hobbs' assistant, Jay. I was given this address to find her."

"Jay, me old son," Vic announced from behind Eddie, "How goes it?"

"I'm sorry, how goes what?" Jay frowned.

"You need a lesson in our lingo," Vic chuckled.

"Oh," Eddie smiled again, "you must have meant Lisa." He moved back so that Jay could enter the house.

Vic led him through the house and into the living room where Mason sat with a sleeping Ethan. Jay shot him a concerned gaze as Mason stood to greet him.

"Jock's boys rammed dirty screwdrivers into his legs, poor kid," he explained with a growl.

"I'm sorry, who is Jock again?" Jay asked looking slightly befuddled.

"Jock is the one who seems to have your boss by his short and curlies." Vic replied. Jay smiled, he understood that. "You may know him as Mr Mackenzie."

Jay nodded, "Yes, Mr Mackenzie, I know who you mean now."

Vic raised his eyebrows at Mason, "Lisa is upstairs, I'll go and get her for you."

"Thank you," Jay nodded and watched Vic leave the room.

"Park your arse then, son." Mason grinned sitting back on the chair. Jay just stared at him, "Have a seat, take a load off…" he elaborated while rolling his eyes. Jay nodded and sat on the loveseat.

"Would you like a cup of Rosie?" Uncle Eddie asked.

"Now *that* I do know, no thank you" Jay smiled politely, "I have just finished a bottle of soda in the car."

Vic tapped gently on Lisa's door, she lifted her face from her tear soaked pillow and wiped her cheeks with the heel of her hands. Her eyes stung and her face felt stick. She blew her nose into a tissue and opened the door, Vic smiled sympathetically,

"Jay's here to see you, love," he told her softly. "Are you alright?"

"Yes," she tried to smile, but her face wouldn't move. "I'll be down in a minute."

"Okay," Vic nodded and turned from her. "For the record, Lisa, I am a pretty good judge of character and I honestly don't think Mark is all bad."

"Trust me to fall for a liar, eh," she shrugged, "anyway, I won't be long." She promised.

After washing her face, she slowly stomped down the stairs. Jay stood upon her entering the living room and held out his hand.

She glanced at her uncle who gave a wry smile and shook his hand, "Nice to meet you," she muttered.

"And you, uh, Lisa, right?"

She heaved in a breath and nodded, "So, what do you have to tell me?" she asked perching on the edge of the arm of the couch, where Ethan still slept.

"It's about Mark," he replied sitting back on the chair and leaning forward resting his elbows on his beige chinos. "I think he has gone out of his mind."

"Well, that has nothing to do with me anymore," she shrugged.

"He said you would say that when I told him I was coming to see you." He smiled slightly. "He has cleared out all of his accounts, business and personal alike, he literally has nothing left in the bank."

"Why?" she frowned.

"He has gone to London to confront Mr, um, I mean, Jock, he is giving him everything he has in return for your freedom and to leave you to live in peace."

"What?" she demanded and stood from the arm, pain shot through her body, Jock would kill him, he killed Ben and now he was going to kill Mark.

"He couldn't bear to let Jock hurt you ever again. So he is going to beg for your life by giving Jock his own life."

She shook her head, this was insane, crazy, heat raged her body and her head began to fizz,

"Bloody idiot," Mason spat from behind her, "why would the dozy plonker go and do something so stupid?"

"Because the *dozy plonker* is in love with her," Jay retorted.

"Oh, my God," she couldn't comprehend this, Ben was dead, now Mark would be dead because of her, because she wanted a better life. "What time is his flight?" she asked weakly.

"He boarded about an hour ago," Jay replied.

"Oh, no," she shook her head feeling sick, he had called her before going, before leaving to give his life for her, he called to apologize and she more or less hung the phone up on him. "We have to go, we have to stop him."

"I was hoping you would say that and took the liberty of getting tickets for the next flight to London."

"Hold on a minute, you're acting like a bull in a china shop, sunshine," Uncle Eddie frowned. "Number one, I am not allowing my niece to go on a rescue, suicide mission with someone who can't even tie up shoe laces," he groaned and pointed at Jay's unlaced shoe, "Number two, how do we know that this isn't just a ploy to lure us back to London and number three, no one ever won the race by shooting out of the starting blocks too fast. My old mother used to say you got to learn to walk before you can run. Lisa, this could be a trap and I think it would be bloody stupid to go running after him, he's made his choice…"

"You know what Jock is like," she yelled, "he'll shoot him between the eyes after he takes all of his money and then he'll still come after me," she snapped. "Sorry, but I have to at least try and stop him from making a huge mistake on my behalf."

"What's going on?" Rory asked sleepily.

"Yours truly here has just informed us that Mark has hopped a flight to the Smoke and is about to hand himself over to Jock in exchange for Lisa." Mason explained.

"Arse," he sighed shaking his head. "So, what's the plan?"

"Lisa wants to try and stop him," Eddie spat.

"I am going, none of you can stop me," she left the room and ran upstairs to pack her bag.

Eddie turned to Jay. "If anything happens to her, you will find yourself at the top of my shit list, got it?"

"Yes, sir. It wouldn't be that difficult to get you a ticket too, I am happy to pay for first class." Jay offered.

"Alright, maybe you might find yourself a few steps down from the top," Eddie agreed, "only a few mind." He added. "You sort out three tickets back to London..."

"Three," Jay interrupted.

"These two men saved our lives, they are as dishonest as the day's got twenty-four hours, but they are as loyal as a dog and I ain't going anywhere without them. They know their shit, they believe Jock is wrong and I trust them with mine and Lisa's life. They will have our backs, plus they know where to find Jock. Do we have a deal?" Eddie asked.

"I will get on it now, sir," Jay promised and lifted his cell to his ear.

She hated leaving Ethan alone while recovering from his injuries, but he was not well enough to travel and after a quick call to Dr Munroe, begging her to drop in on him over the next few days, they left for the airport.

Vic and Mason hadn't said anything about the speech Eddie had given Jay about them, but both felt pretty honoured to be regarded in such a way as Eddie had depicted. Yes they would have his back and they both would protect Lisa if it came to it. Now they were going home and Jock would be surprised to say the least.

Lisa fumbled with her fingers as she sat next to her Uncle. It was the first time she had ever flown first class and liked the huge comfy seats along with extra room, especially as she was expanding and would need the extra space.

Mason and Vic wanted to keep their wits about them so refused the complimentary champagne as they waited for take-off. Neither of them liked the idea of facing their wives, they knew all too well that both would have sharpened their nails and either of them could be sleeping on the other's couch the following night.

The flight was long, a full ten hours until they landed at Gatwick airport. They waited for Jay and Lisa, as Holly, because that was all the identification she had, to clear immigration and then they took a taxi to Eddie's flat in Peckham. Mason and Vic called their wives and got an earful for not calling sooner and luckily, Eddie's wife, Maggie, was at her regular hair appointment. The flat was empty and Lisa was able to take a shower before they decided what to do next.

Jay was not impressed by his first impression of London, all he had seen was housing estates and cars on the wrong side of the road. He worried for his friend and wondered how he would find his way around, while sat watching the news on the television and sipping Eddie's take on the perfect cuppa. Too scared and polite to refuse, he gagged down the tea that he had added three teaspoons of sugar to in a hope to make it taste better. It didn't, but he didn't want to risk offending any of them.


Lisa emerged from the shower, refreshed, but still tired. She knew full well she'd never be able to rest until Mark was safe again. So, she had a cup of tea and asked if Mason would try and see if he could set up some sort of meeting with Jock.

Mason thought it would be a better idea to ask Julian instead, in case Jock had got wind of them jetting off to the States to protect Lisa.

"Hello?" he said.

"Julian, it's Mason, mate, how are ya?"

"Not good." He replied bluntly.

"Why?"

"My uncle found out I warned you, I am in St. James' hospital at the moment with no knee caps, so, thanks for that."

"I didn't tell him, son, I am sorry you are hurt."

"I know, look, if you are looking for him, he's meeting some Yank at the docks at twelve today."

"Which docks?" Mason asked looking at his watch, it was already ten-fifteen.

"East India, is she alright? Did you find her?"

"She's safe, for now." Mason replied.

"Least I know it was worth it."

"I feel bad about you getting hurt." Mason moaned.

"Don't, just do me a favour, when you find him, hit him for me, arsehole couldn't even shoot my knee caps out himself, he got one of his Muppets to do it."

"I got it, I'll come and see you later, get Vic to bring you in some grapes."

"That would be pucka, mate, bloody grub in here is utter crap, honestly, I think the dogs at Battersea get fed better than we do."

"In that case, I will go and see my old mate at the greasy spoon on the corner of my street and bring you some steak and kidney pie and mash." Mason promised, feeling bad for Julian's condition.

"Now you are making me feel hungry, cheers, mate."

"Don't mention it, see you later." Mason said and ended the call.

He returned to the others and explained what Julian had told him. It angered Vic to think the kid was suffering because his own uncle didn't give a toss about anyone but himself.

Eddie, not liking what he had heard, contacted an old colleague for a certain someone's phone number, then he called Jock, and explained who he was. He didn't need to tell him much, Eddie Riggler's reputation was still the talk of the East End, when Jock began to wind him up he snapped, "Listen to me, you don't sound to me like you are playing with a full deck, mate, I was running the streets before you were out of nappies and still feeding off your mother. I don't take too kindly to you trying to kill me or my niece. I have something you want and if you ever want to see these pretty, little ladies again, you will listen to everything I have to say."

"She stole from me," Jock barked.

"No, Ben stole from you, she was just his donkey. Ben paid you back with his life, you lost, Jock, you lost and you hate that, don't ya?"

"Listen to me, old man, your niece is a thief and thieves need to be punished. I can't get to her, so I will start on her new boyfriend here, then I will head down to Bournemouth and pay her Nan, mother and wee brother a visit."

"You touch one hair on my sister's head and I swear to you, *mate*, your balls will be knocked into your throat." Eddie growled.

Jock was silent for a few moments, he didn't like being spoken to in this way, much less having his balls threatened, but he wanted his stones, more than anything, more than revenge on Lisa, he wanted to see his diamonds. "Tell you what, *mate*, you bring me my gems and I will see that no one comes to any harm." Jock retorted.

"Alright, when and where?"

"Warehouse two-seventy on Jamestown Way, two o'clock, we'll be waiting."

"Two o'clock and I mean it, this ends today." Eddie warned.

He hung up the phone and turned to the others, Lisa looked sick, her hands were shaking and she shook her head.

"I need to go and see a few of my friends," Mason stated, "Vic and me will get the hard-wear and we'll meet you back here at half-past-one, alright?"

"Thanks," Eddie nodded. "Lisa, I think you need to stay here, I can get a couple of boys from the gym to sit with you."

"No, he won't stop hunting me down, if I face him he'll either kill me or let me go, right?" she replied adamantly.

Eddie didn't like it and as much as he wanted her safe and out of the way, he knew his words were falling on deaf ears. She was as stubborn as her Nan and he knew it was a battle he'd never win.

Margaret returned from having her hair done and was so pleased to see Eddie was home, though she was a little unsure of Jay, she hugged Lisa and made them all bacon sandwiches. It had been years since Lisa had seen her great aunt and was so relieved to see that she hadn't changed much at all.

They talked about the baby and made idle conversation and she grilled Jay as the hours wound down on the clock and it grew closer to the time they had to leave.

To get Maggie safely out of the way Eddie gave her the money to go to bingo for the afternoon with her friends.

When Vic and Mason returned, they left for the docs. Eddie had pre-arranged to meet two others, when they got nearer to the docs. He knew Jock would have reinforcements and figured that it couldn't hurt to have a few of his own. He didn't know this, but Vic and Mason had done the same, just in case it got out of hand.

# Eighteen

They stopped Vic's Jag outside of the red brick warehouse on the East India docs. The sun shone brightly from above in a pure blue sky and sea gulls swooped towards the lapping waves on the side of the quay.

They all looked around and with the sound of a few cranes and the distant bellow of boat horns, the docks were reasonably quiet. The warehouse looked empty, of course it was empty, Jock only used it to administer torture to people, pull off a few fingernails, that sort of thing. So he wouldn't have and goods there.

Lisa took a nervous gulp of air and flashed her eyes at Jay who had lost all of the colour from his face. Uncle Eddie's men approached after climbing out of a dark grey Mercedes and shook his hand and then handed him what looked like to be a bag of powder. The taller of the two men had a warm friendly smile except for one thing, his teeth were all gold. His shoulders were broad and he must have been six feet seven at least. His friend was very stocky and had a wide neck. He had no hair on his head that shone in the afternoon sun. He had a blond moustache that edged is mouth and grew down to his square jaw.

"This is Martin, Hammer Fist, Pardy," Eddie introduced the taller of the men, "and Gary Barking Mad, Barker," he added pointing to the other man. Both nodded their heads and smiled slightly.

"Haven't seen you for a while," Vic said shaking hands with Barker.

"Nah, Wandsworth had the pleasure of my company for a few months, must like me there, they keep asking for me to go back."

"Usual?" Vic asked.

"You know me, mate," Barker grinned revealing he had a tooth missing at the front. "Don't worry, treacle," he then smiled at Lisa, "We'll get this sorted out." She nodded her head.

A blue Ford Mondeo drove around the corner and two more men got out, looking a bit younger than all of them, one had carrot red hair and the other had blond, cut short and spiked on top with a jar of hair gel in it.

"Paul," Mason smiled, "thanks for coming, mate."

"Anything to send Jock back to where he come from, Mason." The red haired grinned adamantly. "I told Bobby here and he was like, count me in." he winked.

"Bobby, how's the baby?" Vic asked.

"Starts school in September, Vic, not such a baby anymore."

"They don't stay babies for long, son." Vic smiled.

Eddie stepped forward, "Are we ready, lads? You know the plan, no one uses a shooter unless it's completely necessary, we get the Yank and we give Jock a message, got it?"

"Got it," they all agreed, Lisa frowned as they handed each other guns, loaded them and hid them under their shirts.

"Let me go in first," Eddie said, "Bobby and Paul, if you don't mind can you go up that fire escape and keep an eye from above?"

"Sure, mate," they nodded and headed towards the side of the building.

Eddie then turned to the others, "Are we ready?" he asked. They all nodded and Lisa drew in an anxious breath.

Eddie banged twice on the painted blue, wooden door. Shortly after, it was slid across and a tall, heavy set man in a tan, brown, leather jacket frowned at them all.

"We're here to see Jock." Eddie told him.

"Just you and the girl, no one else gets in." he groaned.

"Alright," Eddie gave him a wry smile and turned away from him, he didn't like how this felt and decided that if one goes in, they all get in. "Come on then lads, let's go."

"Hold up," he called out, they turned back towards him. "You can come in, but no shooters."

"We don't have any shooters," Eddie lied.

"Pull the other one, it's got bells on it," the man smirked. Eddie looked at Martin and Gary, they took hold of his leather jacket and dragged him out of the way. Lisa watched as they marched him to the edge of the docks,

Martin head butted him in the face and then they tossed him into the Thames.

When they returned they both smiled, "Let's go then," Pardy said confidently.

Eddie led them inside and they headed towards the main part of the warehouse, tied to a chair, unconscious and covered in blood, sat Mark. His head was lowered and his white shirt stained red. Three men stood in front of him, one shorter than the other two,

"I might have known you two idiots would be in on this," the middle man snarled at Vic and Mason, his accent was raw, he was Jock. Lisa pulled a disgusted face at him, the men either side of him were the two that had beaten Ben to death. Her insides tightened and she tried very hard to hide her swollen bump from him, he noticed, of course, "So, congratulations are in order." He mocked.

"Cut the turd talk," Eddie growled. "I thought you promised not to harm Mark."

"I did, but I can't speak for my men, speaking of which, where is Stan? He was on the door."

"He pen and inked a bit," Pardy smiled smugly, "so we decided he needed to take a bath in the drink."

Jock shook his head, "I thought we were going to talk business, not kill each other off."

"The thing is, Jock," Eddie stepped forward, "I am a reasonable man, I was always prepared to come to the table with an offer, but now you have beaten this poor sod within inches of his life, well, I am not sure I want to deal with you anymore."

"Give me my gems and I will let you all leave, no come backs, no aftermath, just a clean deal." Jock pressed.

"I was prepared to make a deal with you, but look at him," Eddie frowned pointing to Mark. He had begun to swing his head from side to side, "And I suppose you have his money."

Jock smiled like a kid caught with his fingers in the biscuit tin, "I have had to fork out a lot of dough for this, I need to recoup some of my expenses back."

"You give him back his money and I will give you back your ladies, simple as that."

"Can I see them?"

"Lisa," Eddie turned to her, she held out the black velvet bag of diamonds.

"No, I want to see my gems." Jock snapped. She poured some of the diamonds into her hand and his face lit up. He nodded towards one of the men stood behind him and he lifted Mark's briefcase, bringing it to Jock. "So, how are we going to do this?"

"Well, first I want to hear you apologise to my niece, you killed her boyfriend and left her alone, so, Jock, say you are sorry." Eddie explained confidently.

"Up yours, granddad, I am not apologising, he stole from me." Jock barked.

"No apology, no deal," Eddie shrugged.

"Okay, sorry, Lisa, sorry Ben was a stupid prat who dragged you into this and left you to face the consequences." He stepped towards her, "Sorry he was a jumped up little twat who thought he was smarter than me, cleverer than I could ever be, well, he lost, I won, I always win."

"Not always," she frowned.

"What?"

"Well, I sold half the diamonds, so I only have half here, plus your thugs you sent for me in Vegas, they're toast now, so you don't always win Jock. You just think you are better than everyone else and no one means anything to you. All you want is more money at whatever cost, as long as you win." She spat.

"I don't think I am better than anyone else, I am better than everyone else." He boasted. "As for you two," he pointed to Vic and Mason, "Poplar is not your home anymore, you have twenty four hours to get your tart wives and get the hell out of my town."

"Your town?" Vic growled and charged towards him, both his men were at his side in seconds. He stopped and stepped back slightly.

"We are not alone, I have men all over this place," at that second two loud bangs echoed out, a man fell from the metal walkway and landed in a dead heap on the ground.

"So do I," Eddie smiled. Jock's face took on a grave expression, "That was for Ben." Eddie added.

"The only person leaving London is you," Mason roared.

"I own this town," Jock stated shaking his head and pulling a gun out from behind him, he pulled Mark's head up and pushed the barrel of the gun into his temple. "Give me my gems and no one else has to die."

Lisa went to step forward, Eddie took hold of her arm, "Hold up, love," he told her. "Now you listen to me, Jock. Put the gun away and we will make a deal."

"Seems to me you don't understand my lingo, am I not speaking the Queen's English for you, laddie? Can you not understand my orders? Give me my bloody diamonds or I put a bullet through his skull, got it?" Jock's two men moved towards them, two bangs echoed out from above and both of them hit the floor, dead.

Mason, Vic, Gary and Pardy pulled out their guns and aimed them at Jock. Jay moved next to Lisa and pushed her behind him.

"Step away from the boy," Eddie said calmly. "You have no one left, Jock, step away and we can end this." Jock's eyes darted frantically around the room, then he smiled sadistically…

Bang!

A bullet landed in the middle of his forehead, they all looked at each other, no one had fired a gun.

Eddie spun around, a young lad on crutches held a smoking gun out in front of him.

"Julian," Vic smiled. "You are meant to be in hospital."

"Well, I wanted to show my uncle I could do one thing right, I could shoot the arsehole and not miss."

"Yes you did, well done, son," Vic said tucking his gun into the back of his trousers.

"We need to get out of here, there's a gas leak," Julian suggested.

Lisa shook her head, "I can't smell gas."

"It's time to go, treacle," Pardy said putting his arm over her shoulder, "its over." She nodded and he escorted her out. Uncle Eddie filled Jock's pockets with the white powder and saved enough to sprinkle on the ground by Jock's car, if nothing else, it would look like a drug deal gone wrong.

Jay and Vic helped Mark up and took him out to the car. With his briefcase full of cash beside him on the back seat, he passed out again. Jay explained that he thought he should get looked at and Vic and Mason said they would take him to the hospital. Paul and Bobby emerged and they all drove down the street.

# Nineteen

Climbing out of the cars Lisa turned to them, she emptied the diamonds into her hand.

"A lot of people have died because of these, and I don't want any part of them anymore, she took a few of them and gave some to Vic, the same to Mason, and so on, sharing them out between them all except Mark, Jay and herself. "Thank you all for your help, I am really grateful."

"I don't need these," Eddie grumbled.

"Yes you do, take Aunt Maggie away or something," she insisted, "I can't thank you enough."

"If you are sure," Vic frowned.

"I am sure, you more than earned them, I have all I need. All I want now is to go and see my mum."    They all thanked her knowing that each diamond was worth between fifty and a hundred grand, none of them would need to worry about money again.

They then watched as Pardy shot a bullet at the open gas pipe and the warehouse exploded. A ball of flames roared into the sky, sirens and alarms rang out as they said their goodbyes. Eddie shook hands with Bobby and Paul before they left. Then with Pardy and Barker, they climbed into their E180 and drove off.

Vic and Mason hugged Lisa and asked that she let them know when she'd had the baby. She agreed, though wanting to put all of this behind her, she had no clue as to what she would do next. She couldn't keep her eyes off Mark though, they needed to talk, but she was too scared to let him go.

"It was nice working with you boys," Eddie told them shaking their hands.

"Likewise, mate," Mason nodded, "If you are ever looking for something on the side, I wouldn't mind teaming up with you again."

"I am in retirement, but if you ever need me, you know where to find me." Eddie smiled warmly.

"We'll take Mark to the hospital," Vic promised. "You ever play golf, Eddie?"

"Nah, best way to ruin a good walk, me old son," Eddie chuckled.

"That's what I say," Mason grinned.

"I do like a bit of boxing though, maybe we can get our boys together for a knock about in the ring sometime."

"You're on," Vic grinned.

Lisa watched as they drove off leaving just her and her uncle, she should have at least said goodbye to Mark. But in her heart she felt it better to have a clean break, now he could get on with his life and she could start to enjoy her pregnancy.

They could see the smoke from the balcony of her uncle's flat. Black clouds bellowing into the turquoise sky, she watched it while sipping tea and waiting for her taxi to take her to the train station. She was going home, she still had a few diamonds left and planned on giving them to her family.

While she waited, her uncle called the Jersey police and claimed Ben's body, saying he was the uncle of his girlfriend and they wanted him back. In Ben's passport he had put Lisa as his next of kin and the police agreed to have him shipped to the mainland, though they would have to cover the cost.

If he couldn't make sure Lisa's baby had a father, he would at least ensure that the baby would have a grave to visit.


Before she left for the station, Eddie's phone rang, "I can only ask her," he muttered. She turned to face him, "Mark is asking for you to visit him in hospital, he is going back to Houston tomorrow."

"I can't," she sighed.

"You'll regret it, love, I know how much he means to you."

"Sorry, but no," she stated and stood lifting her bag from the floor. "I will call you when I get to my mum's."

"Alright, love, take care." He said softly and she left. She couldn't go and say goodbye to Mark, she didn't want to see him leave her behind.

She arrived at Bournemouth train station as the BBC news was reporting a huge fire on the docks in London. It made her shudder to think of what they might find there and what everyone had done for her. But she was relieved to be going home.

She knocked on her mum's front door and waited. Nick pulled the door open and threw his arms around her neck, pulling into his body. They had been informed by Nan of everything that had happened, so her mum and Nick were expecting her home, they just weren't expecting her to be pregnant.

They talked over a cup of tea and she explained that Ben's body would be arriving at a funeral parlour in town ready to be cremated. Her mum held her as weeks of anguished left her body, she sobbed on her mother's shoulder, relieved to be safe and free, but also afraid of what the future would hold for her now.

After she had pulled herself together she asked if she could call Ethan and explain that she wouldn't be coming back.

"Why aren't you going back?" her mother asked.

"I can't, can I?"

"Of course you can, and Nick and I will come and see you," she replied.

"I was meant to start a life there with Ben, well, he is going to be here, this is my home."

"Home is where you lay your hat, you know that, love," her mum stated.

"I thought you'd be happy to have me back," she grumbled.

"We are, only, we think you are bloody stupid to leave your house over there." Nick offered.

She thought about his words, yes, it would be so easy to just go back and move on with her life, but Lisa never chose the easy option, ever.

"I am not going anywhere until I have laid Ben to rest," she said finally and left the kitchen.


She was relieved to hear Ethan's voice and happy that the house was still in one piece. He said that he and Dr Munroe, or Shelly as he called her, had gotten on quite well and he was considering asking her out on a date. After chatting with him for a while, she went to her room and collapsed on her bed. Remembering the last time she was there, the conversations she had with Ben about their future. She placed her hand on her bump and felt the baby move inside, wondering if she would enjoy life in Texas more now that she didn't have to hide, that she was finally free, free of Jock and free of the diamonds.

Uncle Eddie called the following day to say that Ben's body would be arriving that morning and the funeral home had managed to get the next available funeral at the crematorium the following afternoon. Because Ben was not in a good shape they needed to get his cremation done as quick as possible.

Uncle Eddie also informed her that he and Mason had been interviewed by the police with regard to the warehouse fire where five lots of remains were more or less incinerated. The gas explosion was so hot, they were only really able to recover teeth. As his car was caught on CCTV the police wondered why he was in the area. Eddie told her she had nothing to worry about and everything was taken care of.

The following day, Lisa dressed in a black dress, Nick wore a suit and her mum and Nan also wore black dresses, they all rode in silence in the back of a limousine. She didn't like the idea of a cremation, but it was quick and it meant that she could try and rebuild her life. She also dreaded the fact that there would be hardly anyone there. Ben had no family and the few friends she told were all in London.

As they climbed out of the limousine she was elated to see Eddie with Maggie, Mason and Vic, Bobby and Paul and Gary stood with Martin and Julian. As she approached them Eddie opened his arms and hugged her, then he hugged his sister and niece.

"I can't believe you all came," she sniffed looking at Mason.

"Ben was one of us, love."

"Thank you," she smiled slightly.

The hearse carrying Ben's body in a dark wood coffin, rolled up and stopped with a screech of the breaks. The funeral director got out and asked for Lisa, she stepped forward.

"We have done all you have asked with regards to the service," he explained in a soft voice, she gazed into his grey eyes and nodded.

She had spent an hour or more on the phone with them arranging some sort of service for the man she once loved. She was amazed by the amount of flowers surrounding the coffin, looked at her uncle and he winked. Of course he had ordered them and she was relieved that her heart shaped wreath was not the only flowers he had.

"It's time," the directed said, "are you ready?" she nodded her head and they lifted Ben's coffin out of the back of the hearse. She followed with her uncle at one side and Nick the other. They carried him in to the song 'Demons' by the band Imagine Dragons, Ben's favourite band. It was his favourite song and sung it to her all the time. The words danced on her spine now, *'When the days are cold and the cards all fold, and the saints we see are all made of gold...'* He loved that song and the words seemed more significant now, *'It's where my Demons hide.'* Tears dripped off her chin as she was shown to a seat and waited for everyone else to enter.

The Chaplin was very kind about a man he had never met. The words he used were soothing and though she cried, she couldn't forget that the whole reason she was now left with a fatherless child was because he got greedy.

After the service they lowered his coffin to ground level and she tossed a red rose on top of his name as she left the chapel closely followed by her mum and brother. Outside they had laid the flowers so she could view them.

"Lisa," Eddie said quietly at her side, "there is someone here to see you." She nodded, wiped her tears with a tissue and turned around, Mark smiled humbly.

"Are you okay?" he asked softly.

"Yes," she nodded, but her eyes filled with tears and spilled over, "sorry," she sniffed and wiped them with her now soggy tissue. "I thought you were going home."

"I am not leaving without you," he replied. She looked at her mum who grinned, "Sorry, bad timing and all of that, but, I just thought that maybe we could..."

"You lied to me," she frowned.

"I know and I'm sorry," he sighed. "Look, we need to talk, really talk," he placed his hand on her arm, she looked at his hand and frowned, "sorry," he muttered and removed it. "Can we talk?"

Her mum stepped towards them, "Sorry, love, but uh, shall we invite everyone back to ours? I wasn't expecting to hold a wake, but I don't mind, I am sure I can make some sandwiches."

"Sure, Mum, thanks. Oh, this is, this is Mark, my uh…friend from Texas."

"Nice to meet you, Mark," she smiled and held out her hand.

"And you, ma'am," he smiled shaking her hand.

"Call me Jennie. You'll come back to ours, won't you?"

"If it's alright with Lisa, then yes, Jennie, thank you, that would be nice."

"Of course," Lisa agreed and shortly after they left in a convoy back to her home.

Lisa thanked the funeral directors as the Limo dropped them off and they went inside. Nick ran to the shop to get some more milk, bread and crisps, so that they could at least offer some food to these men who had travelled down from London.

Lisa led Mark outside to the back garden and they sat on garden chairs, under the parasol talking.

"Come back with me," he pleaded for the third time.

"I can't, Mark. I don't know if I can trust you anymore for one thing."

"I am still me," he offered. She drew in a deep breath. "I will never lie to you again, I will be honest and upstanding, I will look after you and provide a life for the baby. You'll want for nothing."

"I don't need anything," she replied sourly. He could see she wasn't convinced.

After an hour or so, Jay appeared at the back door and said that they had to leave. Their flight was that night and they had to get back to London.

They said their goodbyes and she walked with him out to the waiting cab.

"Well, if you change your mind…" he began.

"I won't," she frowned and swallowed hard on the lump of emotion forming in her throat.

"Just in case you do, you know where to find me."

"Okay," she nodded. Before she could say anything he folded his strong arms around her and held her close to his thudding heart,

"Thank you for coming to my rescue," he said into her hair.

"It was the least I could do," she muttered as he pulled back from her. He placed his lips against her forehead and kissed her tenderly before leaving her arms, he opened the car door, "I will miss you, Holly Long." He declared.

"I'll miss you too," she admitted. He closed the door and the cab drove away. She stood on the street outside of her house and watched it drive around the corner, disappearing out of site, like Mark had disappeared from her life.

She returned to the house and her mother was washing up in the kitchen. From the living room she could hear Mason tell of his adventure with the police, she lifted the tea-towel and began to dry the cups.

"Mark is a nice boy," her mother finally said.

"He is," Lisa agreed.

"So, are you going out?"

"Not really," she shrugged and placed the cup on the kitchen side.

"Love, I can see he likes you and that you like him, so what's the problem?"

"I can't trust him," she replied. Her mum frowned, "He let me down, he used me, lied to me and then goes and gets himself almost bloody killed, I can't have that anymore, not around me or the baby."

"He tried to put it right, Lis, he is a nice man, you could do a lot worse."

"So, what happens if I go over there and hurts me again, what do I do then?" she demanded angrily.

"At least you could say you tried, this way you have no idea if its going to work and trust me, you will always wonder what if." Her mum took the towel from her and dried her hands. "I would be happy knowing you are over there with him, happy and safe."

"What about you and Nick?"

"As soon as Nick heard you were in Texas, he was planning on coming to see you, we'll save up, it would be nice…"

"I almost forgot," Lisa said and opened her handbag. She pulled out the small velvet bag which once held the diamonds, she reached inside and pulled out five diamonds. "These are worth about a hundred grand each, I want you to have them."

"What would I do with that sort of money, love?"

"Buy a house, take a holiday…"

Her mum shook her head, "I don't need them, I have all I need. You put them somewhere safe, you never know when they might come in handy."

"Please, Mum,"

"Alright, I'll take one, that way I can make out I found it, but on one condition." Lisa frowned. "You go back to Texas and be happy."

"But?"

"I mean it, Lisa, I want you to go and make a life for yourself, Mark is a good man and I know he will look after you both. Plus I can come and see you whenever I want." She winked.

"Well, I'll have to see if there is a flight," she frowned.

"You just need to catch Mark up, he has a ticket for you already booked." Her mum smiled and hugged her. "Go and live your life."

She put the diamonds back into her handbag and went upstairs to pack the few things she had bought with her, Ethan would be happy to see her. She told herself over and over again. When she came down the stairs Uncle Eddie and Aunt Maggie were ready to leave,

"Come on, Cinderella," he said to her, "let's go and catch Prince Charming up."

She shed a few tears saying goodbye to them all and promised to stay in touch before climbing into Eddie's Jag.

As they drove down the street she glanced back at her family, Vic and Mason waved, Nick had promised that he would be over soon and her mum blew her a kiss as they drove away.

This was it now, for keeps, she had a whole new life to live and though the thought of being with Mark scared the life out of her, she knew deep down everyone was right, he would look after her and the baby.

# Epilogue

The sun blinded her as she stepped out onto the bright green lawn. As she walked towards him, he gave a huge smile. Her heart sped up and beat heavily against her rib cage as she slowly approached him. She glanced around and saw her Nan and her mum, smiling with tears in their eyes, Ethan and Shelly, holding hands. Uncle Eddie walked at her side and as the music began, everyone stood.

Mark was wearing a white suit with a matching tie, at his side stood Jay, who was also in a white suit. As she got closer she felt the baby kick inside of her, to her side she saw her brother bouncing a toddler on his lap, her son, Benjamin Daniel Hobbs was the spit of his father, though everyone thought that was Mark. He had been there from before Ben was born and even suggested the name, now she was carrying a little girl and they couldn't wait for her to arrive.

The sun shone down on them as they sealed their three year relationship with gold bands and promises, this was her happy ending, finally she could breathe.

In London, Vic and Mason now ran a legit car sales bought with the money they had made from finding a few diamonds. Julian now ran a comic shop in Piccadilly. Gary and Martin spent a lot of time in Scotland playing golf and Bobby emigrated to Malta with his wife Mandy and their daughter. Paul got silly with his diamonds and ended up getting ripped off by some Russian mobsters, he now worked at the car sales with Vic and Mason, it was the least they could do.

"Vic, me old mate," Mason gleamed, "Charlie is making me a Granddad."

"Nice one, mate, now when anyone calls you a granddad, you will actually be one. Always said you are on your way to a pipe and slippers," Vic laughed.

"Ha, Ha, bloody, ha," Mason chuckled.

The End

M J Rutter grew up in the seaside town of Bournemouth, Dorset on the south coast of England. She currently lives with her husband and two children in Poole, Dorset. After studying at the New Hampshire Art Institute in 1997, while working as a nanny in America, she returned to the UK and has lived there since.

Other Books

Shadows Lost

Back To Innocence

I, Immortal the Series, Bk 1

Lessons in Love

Lunar Ryce, Soul Collector

Lunar Ryce, Soul Searcher

Summer Rain

Cruel Winter

Coming soon

I, Immortal Bk 2, World in Flames

Lunar Ryce, Soul Saviour

You can find all of Melissa's work on Amazon.

You can follow Melissa on Twitter @MelissaJRutter
On Facebook https://www.facebook.com/MelissaJRutter

For more information on future releases please visit
MelissaJRutterAuthor.webs.com

Made in the USA
Lexington, KY
30 September 2014